"I'm sorry."

Delia's voice was scratchy and soft. The sound of it ran over Max's sensitized skin like a caress.

"It's hardly your fault." He couldn't look at her just now, the words he'd never said still echoing in his head like gunfire. He continued to put away his tools, wishing she'd leave. That she'd never come here.

"Max." He ignored her. Needed to. Should have all along.

But then she touched him. He whirled around and did what he'd longed to do. He slid his hand into the silk of her hair, brushed his thumb against her lips and felt the heat of her startled breath.

She didn't pull away.

"Go," he told her, his fingers tangled in the strands of her fiery hair. "Leave."

She shook her head. "I'm not scared of you. I know bad men, and you're not a bad man."

He pulled her closer, pressed his lips to her neck and whispered, "You don't know me at all."

Dear Reader,

Welcome back to The Riverview Inn, home of the Mitchell men! I had such a good time writing *A Man Worth Keeping*, my woman-on-the-run, man-in-hiding book. The story started with the idea of two people meeting and instantly being able to see the raw truth about each other. You know how sometimes, no matter how strange, you meet someone and you feel as if you're not strangers? (I had that experience with my good friend Jennifer Kavanaugh, to whom this book is dedicated. She opened her dorm-room door and I felt as though I'd known her my whole life.) I could easily see this happening for Max and Delia.

But the problem with Max and Delia is that as well as they see each other, they've lost sight of themselves. Throw in a wily eight-year-old girl, and the second book of THE MITCHELLS OF RIVERVIEW INN is off to a roaring start.

I look forward to hearing from you! Please check out my Web site at www.molly-okeefe.com.

Happy reading!

Molly O'Keefe

A MAN WORTH KEEPING

Molly O'Keefe

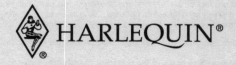

HARLEQUIN®

TORONTO • NEW YORK • LONDON
AMSTERDAM • PARIS • SYDNEY • HAMBURG
STOCKHOLM • ATHENS • TOKYO • MILAN • MADRID
PRAGUE • WARSAW • BUDAPEST • AUCKLAND

ISBN-13: 978-0-373-78231-4
ISBN-10:   0-373-78231-4

A MAN WORTH KEEPING

ABOUT THE AUTHOR

Molly O'Keefe has written eleven books for the Harlequin Superromance, Flipside and Duets lines. When she isn't writing happily-ever-after she can usually be found in the park acting as referee between her beleaguered border collie and her one-year-old son. She lives in Toronto, Canada, with her husband, son, dog and the largest heap of dirty laundry in North America.

Books by Molly O'Keefe

HARLEQUIN SUPERROMANCE

HARLEQUIN FLIPSIDE

HARLEQUIN DUETS

*The Mitchells of Riverview Inn

To the person at Webster University who assigned Jennifer Kavanaugh to the dorm room across from mine. Whoever you are, you changed my life. Thanks.

You're not too shabby either, JK.

PROLOGUE

WAS THAT…a frog?

Max Mitchell tried to clear his vision, but the pain and blood made it impossible. But the frog— if that's what the green blur on the ceiling was— seemed to sway and scream in time with his charging heartbeat.

He was dying, his blood pumping out of his body beneath a flying, screaming frog.

Is this shock?

His brain sent the message to his nerves to lift his hand so he could wipe the blood from his face.

Come on, hand, lift. Here we go.

But it didn't work. The nerves didn't respond.

He spit out the blood that pooled, coppery and hot in his mouth, and groaned from the effort.

The screaming, he realized when his ears suddenly popped, wasn't from the frog. It was from the baby in the crib under the frog. The frog mobile, blood spattered and cockeyed.

Nell picked up the baby and the screaming stopped.

Relief rattled through his body, slowing his heart rate. Or it could be loss of blood. Either way Nell had lived and he was so tired.

"Mitchell!"

Someone called his name and he made the effort to turn his head, but agony screamed through his neck and the black edges of the world closed in.

"Mitchell, can you hear me?"

The frog was replaced by the bearded face of his partner.

Good—Nell, the baby and Anders are still alive.

"You've got a bullet in the groin and it looks like another one creased your neck and cheek." Anders was putting a good face on it, trying to smile, but Max could feel his partner using both hands and all his weight to stanch the blood pouring out of Max's body.

"Hurts."

Anders laughed. "I should think."

"Groin?"

"It's bad, lots of blood. But you'll live to love another day."

"Where—" The blood made it difficult to talk, but he spit out more and tried again. "Where's Tom?"

"Tom?"

"The dad. Adult male."

Anders glanced briefly behind him, where blue shapes and the screaming and the frog all lingered just out of Max's focus.

"The wife is hurt, but not bad. The infant is fine, but we were too late for the dad. The first bullet was right through the chest. He died instantly."

Justice, Max thought, *is too damn complicated.*

Medics approached, pushing Anders out of the way. But Anders wasn't a man easily pushed and he hovered over a medic's shoulder.

Max was glad. He didn't want to die alone.

"The teenager?" Max asked as the medics lifted him onto the stretcher. Hot shards of pain, like glass, like blowtorches and firebombs, blazed up his body from his leg. He screamed, warm blood spilling into his mouth and he choked.

"Jesus, guys. Careful," Anders barked, and the medics ran to get Max out of the nursery room that had turned into a bloodbath.

"The teenager?" he cried, pushing against the black edges that lingered and taunted him with sweet relief.

"You got him," Anders said, pride and regret in his voice. "He's dead."

Max had done his job. He let go and the world went dark.

CHAPTER ONE

Two years later

MAX MITCHELL SLID the two-by-four over the sawhorses and brushed the snow off his hand tools, but more fat flakes fell to replace what he'd moved.

It was only nine in the morning, and the forecast had called for squalls all day.

Winter. Nothing good about it.

Of course, spending every minute of the season outside was a surefire way to cultivate his dislike of the cold. But lately, walls no matter how far away—and ceilings—no matter how high—felt too close. Like coffins.

The thick brown gloves didn't keep out the chill so he clapped his hands together, scaring blackbirds from the tree line a few feet behind him.

Even the skeleton structure he'd spent the past few months constructing seemed to shiver and quake in the cold December morning.

He eyed his building and for about the hundredth time he wondered what it was going to be.

It wasn't one of the cottages that he'd spent last spring and summer building for his brother's Riverview Inn.

Too small for that. Too plain for his brother, Gabe, the owner of the luxury lodge in the wilderness of the Catskills.

Max told everyone it was going to be an equipment shed, because they needed one. But it was so far away from the buildings that needed maintaining and the lawns that needed mowing, he knew it would be a pain in the butt hauling equipment back and forth.

Still, he called it a shed because he didn't know what else to call it.

Besides, the construction kept his hands busy, his head empty. And busy hands and an empty head stymied the worst of the memories.

The skin on the back of his neck grew knees and crawled for his hairline and he whirled, one hand at his hip as if his gun would be where it had been for ten years. But of course his hip was empty and, behind him, watching him silently beneath a snow-covered Douglas fir, was a little girl.

"Hi," he said.

She waved.

"You by yourself?" He scanned the treeline for a parent.

She nodded.

Talkative little thing.

"Where'd you come from?" Max asked.

The girl jerked her thumb toward the inn that was back down the trail about thirty feet through the forest.

"Are you a guest?" he asked, although it was Monday and most guests checked in on Sunday. "At the inn?"

She shrugged.

"You…ah…lost?" Max asked.

She shook her head.

"Can you talk?"

She nodded.

"Are you gonna?"

She shook her head and smiled.

His heart, despite the hours in the cold, warmed his chest.

"Do you think maybe someone is worried about you?"

At that the girl stopped smiling and glanced behind her at the buildings barely visible through the pines.

"Should we head back?" he asked, stepping away from his project in forgetting. At his movement she darted left, away from the trail, under the heavy branches of trees and he stopped.

She was a deer ready to run. And since beyond him there was a whole lot of nothing, he figured he'd best keep her here until someone came looking for her.

"All right," he said. "We don't have to go anywhere."

Amongst the trees, her pink coat partially hidden in shadows, he saw her pink-gloved finger point at the building behind him.

"It's a house," he said.

She laughed, the bright tinkle filling his silent clearing.

"You think it's too small?" he asked, and her head nodded vigorously.

"Well, it's for a very small family—" he eased slightly closer to her where she hid "—of racoons."

Something crunched under his foot and she zipped deeper into the shadows and now he couldn't see her face. He stopped.

Two years off the force and he'd lost his touch.

"Want to play a game?" he asked, and when she didn't answer and didn't run he took it for a yes. "I'm going to guess how old you are and if I guess right, we go inside, because it's too cold." He shivered dramatically.

Again, no sound, no movement.

"All right." He closed his eyes and rubbed his temples. "It's coming to me. I can see a number and you are…forty-two."

She laughed. But when he took a step, the laughter stopped, as if it had been cut off by a knife. He stilled. "What am I—too low? Are you older?"

Her gloved hand reached out between tree limbs and her thumb pointed down. "You're younger?" He pretended to be amazed. "Okay, let me try…eight?"

No laughter and no hand.

For one delightful summer of his misspent youth, Max had been an age and weight guesser on Coney Island. He had a ridiculous intuition for such things and that summer it had gotten him laid more times than he could count.

Ah. Misspent youth.

"Am I right?" he asked.

She stepped out from underneath the tree, her face still, her eyes wary.

"Are you scared? Of going back?"

She shook her head and looked at the end of her bright orange and pink scarf, playing with the tassels.

"You just don't want to?" he asked.

The little girl's eyes lifted to his and he saw a misery there that he totally understood. She didn't like what was back there.

"Tough one," he muttered.

"Josie!" The cry split through the quiet forest. "Josie! Where are you?" It was a woman's voice and she was panicked. Scared.

"You Josie?" he asked the little girl, and her guilty expression was enough.

"She's here!" he yelled. "Stay on the trail and—"

A woman, petite and fair, erupted from the trees and nearly tripped into the clearing. Her wild eyes searched the area until they landed on Josie, small and pink and looking like she wished she could vanish.

"Oh my God!" the woman cried, hurtling herself through snow to practically slide on her knees in front of Josie. "Oh, Josie. I was so worried." She checked the little girl, cupped her cheeks in her own bare hands. The woman didn't even have a coat on.

"What did I say about wandering off?" the woman asked, snow gathering in her red hair. "What did I say? You can't do that, Josie. You can't scare me that way." Finally the woman hauled Josie into her arms but stayed on her knees, her blue jeans no doubt getting soaked through.

No coat. No gloves and now she was going to be wet.

He cleared his throat. "She's been with—"

Before he could even finish, the woman was on

her feet, Josie sequestered behind her. The woman was braced for battle, a bear protecting her cub and Max had serious respect for that particular facet of motherhood and had no desire to screw with it.

He took a careful step away from the two females and lifted his eyes to look into the woman's in an effort to calm her down. He opened his mouth to tell her that he meant no harm, but the words died a quiet death in his throat.

There was a buzz in the air and under his jacket all the hair on his arms stood up.

I know you, he thought, looking into her radiant blue eyes. *I know all about you.* Her stiff shoulders and trembling lips told the tale more vividly than anything she might say. This woman was terrified of more than just losing her daughter momentarily. This was a woman—a beautiful woman—grappling with big fears.

And the big fears seemed to be winning.

Her eyes narrowed and he looked away, suddenly worried that she might see him as clearly as he saw her. Though he didn't know what she would detect in him—cobwebs and dark corners, probably.

"Who are you?" she asked.

"Max Mitchell," he answered calmly, despite the fact that his heart was pumping a mile a minute.

He needed this woman to get out of here. Take her silent daughter and leave.

"Your brother is Gabe? The owner?" He nodded and she relaxed, barely. "He said you were in charge of operations."

"I mow the lawn." He shrugged. "Shovel snow." Not quite the truth, but the fact that just about everything would grind to a halt these days if he wasn't here didn't seem like the kind of thing to discuss at this moment.

"You better head back. You—" He pointed at the wet patches on her jeans and the snow scattered across her bright blue sweater. Her tight, bright blue sweater. A mama bear in provocative clothes, Lord save him. "You are gonna get cold."

And my clearing is getting crowded.

The woman and girl were a pretty picture, surrounded by white snow and green trees. They were bright spots, almost electric seeming. He found it difficult to look away.

"I'm Delia," she said, her accent flavored by the south. Texas, maybe.

A redhead from Texas. Trouble if ever there was. And a woman from Texas without a winter coat or gloves, in a Catskill winter, had to be a guest.

The girl tugged on her mother's hand and Delia wrapped an arm around her.

"And this is my daughter, Josie."

Josie waved a finger at Max and he smiled.

"We're acquainted."

Delia didn't like that. Not one bit. Her lips went tight, and her pale skin, no doubt cold, went red. "We'll head on back. Don't bother yourself showing us the way."

He nodded, knowing when he'd been told to stay put.

They turned toward the trail and Max forced himself not to stare at the woman's extraordinary behind as she walked away.

"What did I say about talking to strangers?" Delia asked.

"I didn't say a word, Mama," Josie said, her voice a quiet peep with enough sass to indicate she knew what she was doing.

Max couldn't help it, laughter gushed out of his throat, unstoppable.

Trouble, the two of them.

DELIA DUPUIS'S mother was French, her father an oil rigger from the dry flatlands of West Texas. Depending on the situation, Delia could channel either of them. And right now, her daughter, her eight-year-old girl who was way too big for her britches, needed a little sample of Daddy's School of Tough Love.

"This isn't funny, Josie," she said. "I don't know that man and he could have been dangerous."

"He was nice," Josie protested.

He was. He was more than nice, and her instincts echoed Josie's statement. But Delia was not on speaking terms with her instincts these days. She had to shake off the strange sensation that she knew Max. Really *knew* him. For a moment there she'd felt a spark of something, like being brushed by electricity, and when she looked into his eyes all she'd thought was, *I can trust this man.*

She'd seen such sadness in his eyes, manageable but there, like a wound that wasn't healing. That sadness and the way he held his head and how he talked to Josie, the way he didn't crowd Delia, the way he had shown her more respect in those five seconds than she'd received in the last year of her marriage, had her whole body screaming that he was one of the good guys.

Which, of course, was ridiculous. She couldn't tell that from a five-second conversation, from a quick glance into a pair of black eyes. And the fact that her instincts told her the compelling, handsome and mysterious man was a good guy was a pretty good indication that he wasn't.

Her instincts were like that.

Delia turned and despite the cold and her aching hands and misleading gut reactions she crouched in front of her daughter. "Listen to me," she said, hard as nails. The smile and spark of defiance fled from Josie's brown eyes. The response killed

Delia, ripped her apart, but she didn't know what else to do. "When I say you stick close, it means you stick close. It means I can see you at all times. I'm not telling you again, Jos. You know how important this is, don't you?"

Josie nodded.

"How important is it?" Delia asked. She would repeat this a million times a day. Delia would tie Josie to her side if she had to.

"It's the most important thing," Josie repeated dutifully.

Delia arched an imperial eyebrow—another trick from her daddy, who could act like a king despite the black under his fingernails.

"Got it?" she asked.

After a moment, Josie nodded, her lips pouty, her eyes on her boots. "Got it."

"I love you, sweetie. I'm just trying to keep you safe."

Delia pulled Josie close, but the child stood unmoving in the circle of her arms.

She just needs more time, Delia told herself, blinking back tears caused by the cold and the unbearable abyss between her and her baby. *She doesn't understand what's going on. She'll come around.*

That's what all the books she'd been reading about raising children after a divorce said. Time, patience and a little control over their own lives were what children needed when growing accustomed to a new divided home life.

And if something in the back of Delia's mind insisted that it couldn't be that simple, she ignored that, too. No one was forking out the big bucks for her thoughts on child rearing, so what did she know?

Only that Josie was too young to comprehend what was happening, all the dangers out there that wanted to tear her away and hurt her. It was Delia's one job—her only mission right now—to keep the dangers away.

"I want my daddy," Josie whispered, her voice filled with tears.

Delia's eyelids flinched with a sudden surge of anger. It was growing harder and harder to control this anger, this ever-bubbling wellspring of rage she had toward Jared.

"I know you do, sweetie," she said, and stood, holding her daughter's small hand in her own.

It was too bad that Daddy was the biggest danger of all.

"Are we going to stay here?" Josie asked as they approached the rear of the beautiful lodge.

"If they give me the job we will."

"Why do you need a job?" Josie asked. "You said we were on vacation."

Delia shrugged. "It's a working vacation. We

won't be here very long." Not that the Mitchell family would know that. They were looking for someone long-term and these days her version of long-term was decidedly shorter than it used to be.

She watched Josie taking in the sights with wide eyes. This was a different world from where they'd come. Snow, pine trees, the towering escarpment of the Catskills—Josie had only seen these things on television. "Do you like it here?"

Josie humphed in response.

"Where will we sleep?" Josie asked, and Delia swallowed hard the guilt that chewed at her. They'd slept in terrible places in the past week and a half. After leaving her cousin's place in South Carolina, she'd been on a slippery slope downward. Afraid to use her credit or debit cards, she'd been forced to use the small amount of cash she had. And small amounts of cash bought them nights in places with bad odors, scratchy sheets and too thin walls.

"In there." Delia pointed to the lodge. "We'll have a room all to ourselves, and we'll each get a bed. And a nice big bathroom with a huge old tub."

And solid locks on the doors.

"How does that sound?" Delia jiggled her daughter's arm, needing just a little help, just a little support, in the brave-face department.

"Good," Josie said, and Delia smiled, the bands of iron that constricted her chest loosened.

"Can I call Dad tonight?"

And like that, she couldn't breathe again.

"Not yet. I told you, sweetie, he's still at that conference. He's going to be there for two whole weeks."

"That's a long time," Josie said, looking glum.

She wanted to comfort her daughter, kiss away the pain that had settled on her small fragile shoulders. But Delia didn't know how.

She didn't know how they were going to get through the day, much less tomorrow or the day after. She'd bought herself a few more days with the lie about Jared being at a conference.

But what then?

Those books she'd read had no answers about this sort of situation and all she had to go on were her faulty instincts.

"Oh, sweetie—" Delia hesitated, reluctant to add another lie to the heaping pile, but knowing she had no choice.

"What?"

"If anyone asks, our last name is Johnson."

MAX SPENT AN HOUR after the females had left his clearing trying to stop smiling. Delia had her hands full with Josie, he thought, cinching on his tool belt then carrying the two-by-fours over to the house.

He slid the wood to the ground and hoped Josie was occupied by something. School. Dance or whatever. Because kids that smart, when left to their own devices, found other ways to occupy their time. And those other ways were never good.

Framing out the roof was a two-person job, but his dad, who had been his primary second throughout the building of all the cabins for the inn, was downstate dealing with his lawyer.

Gabe was useless with carpentry, besides being far too preoccupied acting the nervous husband over his pregnant wife and—

Again, the skin on his neck shimmied in sudden warning that he wasn't alone and he whirled, crouched low, his hand at his hip.

But instead of his standard issue, he had a palm full of hammer.

"Old habits, huh, Max?" Sheriff Joe McGinty stepped into the clearing.

"Careful, grandpa." Max dropped the wood and stepped out of the building, his hand outstretched. "It's getting icy."

"*Grandpa?* Don't make me hurt you." Joe grabbed his hand and shook it mightily. They might have hugged if they were different kind of men. Instead they clapped each other's shoulders and grinned.

"How you doing?" Joe asked, his thin, wrinkled

face chapped by the elements. "Working on your dollhouse."

"It's a shed," Max said, compelled to defend his building. "Want to help me frame out that roof?"

"It's too cold to be working out here." Joe shuddered and rolled up the floppy fur collar on his shearling coat. "Too cold for anything but going inside."

"You come out here to give me a weather report?" Max asked.

Joe ran his tongue over his teeth and appeared to be slightly torn about something, which was more than odd for the old law enforcer. He was like a winter wolf. Scrawny and tough and too stubborn to give up and head for greener pastures. And Max liked him for all those reasons.

"Problems with more kids?" Max asked, pulling his gloves on since it seemed this conversation might take a while.

"Nah." Joe swiped at his dripping nose. "The after-school program you ran out here in the summer set a lot of 'em straight."

Max had had ten kids working here over the summer and fall. Kids who'd gotten in trouble, were failing out of school—some of the worst of them had been headed for the halfway house for teens out by Coxsackie. Two of them still worked here as full employees; no longer the at-risk kids they'd been.

"Sue's still going to school?" he asked about the most stubborn of the kids.

Joe nodded. "She's getting straight D's, but she's there."

"Good," Max said and waited a little longer for Joe to get to the topic he'd traveled out here to discuss.

"You know I've never pried, right?" Joe asked, and Max felt his gut tighten. "I know you were on the force in some capacity. I mean the way you move, the way you keep grabbing for your gun, the way you handle those kids—it tells me you're law enforcement all the way." He paused and Max could feel the old man's eyes on his face.

"You investigating me?" Max asked, kicking snow off his boots, where it had gathered.

"No. That's what I'm saying. I could look you up. Ask around. It wouldn't take much to figure out where you've been."

"So? Why don't you?" Max squinted up into the sky. Here he was outside, no ceiling, no walls. Nothing but trees and clean air and snow. Still, he felt his failure like a weight on his chest. He hauled in a deep breath. Another.

"I keep hoping someday you'll tell me." Joe's voice dropped an octave and was coated in uncomfortable pity.

Max didn't say anything.

"Were you FBI? Undercover? Vice?" Joe asked.

"I was just a cop. That's all."

"I get that it was bad, but—"

"Nothing worse than usual." Max faced Joe and got to the heart of the matter. "Why are you asking?"

"Ted Harris is retiring."

Max smiled. "You're here to celebrate? That idiot's been a thorn in your side for—" Something in Joe's face, a stubborn mix of hope and concern, made Max stop and shake his head. "I don't want the job, Joe."

"Juvenile Parole Officer. You'd be perfect." Joe put his hand on Max's shoulder and Max struggled not to shake it off. Joe continued, "We've got a juvenile crime problem in this county and Ted didn't do jack—"

"I don't want the job, Joe."

"But between the program you ran here and the help you gave me with the break-ins over at the community center, you're perfect. And from what I can gather, you're qualified."

Max nearly laughed. He was qualified. More than qualified. But he was utterly unwilling.

"I don't want the job."

"You like this?" Joe asked, flinging an arm out at the half-built building and the barely visible lodge through the trees. "This is satisfying?"

Max blinked. *Satisfying*. He didn't think in

those terms anymore. This, what he did here with his dad and brother, it was easy. If something went wrong, everyone still woke up in the morning.

Those were the terms he lived by these days.

"Sorry, Joe."

Joe stared at him for a long time and Max avoided his gaze. The guy was too wily and he didn't want or need the man as a surrogate father—he had a great one kicking around. And he didn't need a counselor, or a friend from the force. He needed to be forgotten, left alone.

"I just thought you might be interested. It's a chance to do some real good," Joe said, the disappointment like a neon sign in his voice.

Max couldn't stop the harrumph of exasperated, black humor. He'd been told that once before, three years ago. And maybe he'd done some good—he just didn't care anymore.

"Son—" The pity was back in Joe's voice.

"Gotta frame that roof, Joe. So?" Max faced the old sheriff, kept his eyes empty, his heart bleak. "Unless there's something else you need."

Joe tried to wait him out, no doubt looking for a crack he'd never find.

"Stubborn cuss," Joe grunted.

"I could say the same."

Joe brushed his hands together like he was cleaning Max off of him. A good decision, all in all.

"I'll see you around." Joe tipped his head and turned, heading back up the trail toward civilization.

Max wondered if he'd burned a bridge there. He liked Joe. Liked helping him in the small ways he was willing to take on.

Max opened his mouth to call him back, to apologize or explain why he couldn't take the job. But just the thought of saying the words shut his mouth for him.

He watched Joe walk away until he was replaced by snow, by gray sky, by the isolation Max cultivated like a garden.

CHAPTER TWO

"HI," DELIA SAID to Gabe Mitchell as she entered the dining room from the kitchen, her daughter in tow. "Sorry about the interruption."

"No apologies necessary," Gabe said with a smooth smile. The man had a dangerous charm and was painfully easy on the eyes—a potentially lethal combo and one that in the past would have had her panting at his feet.

Thank God she'd grown up some in the past few years.

From what she could tell, the two brothers could not be more different. Max had been kind enough but she'd bet her car he didn't know how to roll out the red carpet like Gabe. Stupidly, she found herself liking Max's quiet intensity better. But she'd married her husband thinking the same thing and look where that had gotten her.

Delia would make a point to stay away from Max if she landed this job.

"I would have done the same thing if my daughter had run off." Gabe smiled at Josie, who had the good sense to look chagrined.

"Did you see anything interesting?" he asked Josie.

"Max."

Gabe nodded. "Well, he's interesting all right. Did he scare you?"

Yes, Delia thought. *He scares me.*

"No," Josie said. "He was nice."

"Nice?" Gabe pretended to be doubtful. "We're talking about the same guy? Big and tall with black hair and—?"

"That's him." Josie was smiling.

Gabe leaned forward and whispered, "Did he show you his scar?"

Josie's eyes went wide and she shook her head.

Gabe lifted his chin and drew a line across part of his throat. "Pirates got him."

Immediately Josie looked dubious and Delia stifled her own smile. Gabe had just insulted Josie's tenuous status as a big kid.

"There are no such things as pirates." She looked scornful. "You're fooling around."

Gabe sighed and straightened. "You're too smart, Josie Johnson. Too smart for me. I think we've got some coloring books around here somewhere. My wife's idea." Gabe's eyes twinkled.

Ah, yes. The wife.

Smooth smiles or not, there was no way any woman could combat the love Gabe clearly had for his wife, Alice. Delia hadn't met Alice yet, but Gabe's feelings for her practically filled the room.

Gabe turned to the cabinets near the bar to look for the coloring books and Josie rolled her eyes at Delia.

Josie thought she was too old for such things and maybe she was, but Delia lifted her eyebrow anyway. The kid would sit and play with rocks or stare quietly into space or whatever it took for Delia to finish this interview.

They needed this job. They needed it bad. They had no cash and nowhere to go.

Gabe turned around armed with puzzles, books, coloring books and big boxes of crayons and colored pencils.

"After a few dinner-hour disasters, Alice bought this stuff for the guests with kids," he said, handing everything over to Josie, who perked up at the sight of the puzzles.

The girl was a sudoku fanatic.

Josie settled herself at one of the tables and Delia gripped her hands together behind her back, in an attempt to stem the anxiousness whirling through her stomach.

"Where were we?" she asked, while Gabe watched Josie.

"Sorry." Gabe shook his head and laughed. "My wife and I are expecting and I just… It's nuts to think I'm going to have an eight-year-old kid at some point."

He'd told her about the baby maybe a million times when they should have been talking about the inn's new spa services. But Delia smiled. "It goes by fast, that's for sure." She paused for a moment and channeled some of her mother's graceful social niceties. "You were talking about the new addition to the lodge—"

"Right, right. Sorry." Again the lethal smile and she hoped this Alice woman knew how lucky she was. "Follow me." He led her to a door in the back corner of the dining room, next to the elegant desk, where guests checked in. The door had a discreet sign on it: Spa.

"We're still adding the finishing touches, but here it is." He pushed open the door to a dimly lit hallway, painted a soothing gray-green. "There's a little bit of paint and electrical work to do. We wanted to leave it fairly unfinished so whoever we hired could make the space their own."

Delia stood on the threshold and let the chills run through her. Her gut, her head, her heart— they all said, *This is it*.

Daddy always said his momma had the sight. Delia didn't believe in those things anymore—not since Jared had taken a sledgehammer to her life—but she could see herself here. Working. Raising Josie.

This couldn't be a better situation.

Autonomy and security, at least for the time being.

Gabe stepped down the hallway and Delia turned to shoot her willful daughter a look then followed him through the door.

"Our reservations fell so dramatically once the fall colors ended we knew we had to do something." He opened the door to a massage room with a big padded table positioned in the center. There was a shelf for her lotions and even an outlet so she could plug in her hot pot to do hot-stone massages. "We're getting a few cross-country skiers but it's still not enough. So—"

"So, you're an inn and spa."

"Exactly. We were going to wait a few years before adding the spa, but we figured sooner rather than later would help us all keep our jobs." He grinned again and Delia wondered if anyone ever said no to the guy. No wonder his wife was pregnant. "We're ready to start advertising the services, but we wanted to get the right person in, someone who we knew could handle the work and had the right philosophy." Gabe paused, offering her an opportunity to tell him her philosophy.

Funny, she used to have one of those. Now her whole philosophy was surviving the day.

"I was trained in San Antonio," she said. "I apprenticed at the Four Seasons there and am a registered massage therapist and yoga instructor."

"The last month and a bit?" he asked. "You have a gap in your résumé."

Delia forced herself to smile and let the lie slide right off her tongue. "I went to France. Personal reasons."

"Ah, nothing better than personal reasons that lead you to France. Josie must have loved it."

The implication that she must have taken her daughter slid through her like poison. "She did. We both did."

It didn't even faze her anymore, the lies. Her heart didn't trip, her hands didn't go cold, and her face didn't go hot.

She was thirty-seven years old and a liar, now. Another black mark on Jared's hell-bound soul.

"I ran my own business for five years previous to France and at the same time worked at a holistic health center as part of an integrated care system for people suffering from terminal illness."

"That's all right here, Delia." Gabe looked down at his clipboard, where she guessed her résumé was. "I'm hoping to find out a little bit about you. About what you think you can offer and what you think we can offer you."

Right. She felt desperation well up in her gut like sticky tar, clinging to her courage and will, dragging her down to someplace scary.

"I want to be a part of something that people love. Something generous and good," she said, the truth like an elixir, clearing away the fear and despair, the hunger and sleeplessness. Jared used to mock her for thinking she could help people with her "rubdowns." But she'd seen the proof firsthand.

But even as she said the words, they felt like a lie. She hadn't been living a generous life in far too long. Jared's poison had infiltrated her being and she felt small and bitter. So she reached deep into the reasons she'd become a massage therapist, trying hard in this beautiful place to reconnect with the woman she'd once been. "I want to work side by side with people who work hard to do their best, to provide the best experience for guests. I want to help people recover, to feel better, to step lighter and maybe laugh a little more. That's why I loved working at the holistic center. I want to make people's lives a little bit easier—"

"Done. You're hired."

Delia blinked and Gabe laughed. "It's why I

started this inn. I wanted to give people a home away from home and you fit into that perfectly."

She eyed him skeptically. Nothing. *Nothing* in her life lately had been this easy. When she'd read the ad for this position on the Internet, it had read like a dream come true considering her suddenly changed circumstances—seasonal, middle of nowhere, starting immediately.

She'd applied on her first day in South Carolina and the second she got the e-mail from Gabe asking her to come up for an interview, she'd packed Josie into the car and driven north.

Gabe finally shrugged. "Truth is, we haven't had that many applicants. Not many people are excited about living in the Catskills in the middle of winter."

That made her laugh. She wasn't all that excited about it, either. And she certainly never would have come here if she didn't have to. But it would be the last place anyone would look for her. She was a Southern woman, with blood as thin as sweet tea.

"But," he was quick to state, "even if we'd gotten the résumés I do believe you'd still get the job. You're a good fit—I could tell when you walked in. I have instincts about people."

You and me both, buddy. She just hoped he trusted his more than she did her own.

She clenched her hands a bit tighter behind her

back to stop herself from throwing her arms around him.

"I suppose you'd like to know the particulars?" he asked, and she pretended to be interested.

"Of course."

"On paper the salary isn't much but it includes room and board. Tips, of course, are yours. You need to let Chef Tim know of any dietary problems—"

"That's great."

"As per your request, you'll be a contract employee. So no health benefits. Taxes will be your problem. Checks will be made out to Delia Johnson."

"That's no problem." As a contract employee they wouldn't need her social security number and since Delia Johnson didn't have one, that seemed altogether best. She could wait to cash the paychecks—living on tips for as long as she could. She could take a paycheck in and get an ID made, maybe. God, she'd never had to worry about this before.

But with food and lodging covered, all she really needed to pay for was gas and the odds and ends that she and Josie required.

Delia shook her head. She didn't need any more. A roof, food for her daughter, someplace safe for her to catch her breath and figure out what to do next.

"It would be a real pleasure to work here,"

she said. "A real—" *relief, blessing, gift, godsend* "—pleasure."

Gabe held out his hand and Delia put her clammy palm into his. "Welcome aboard, Delia Johnson. We hope you'll stay awhile."

Not likely, she thought, but shook on it anyway.

MAX SHOOK the snow out of his hair and stomped his boots on the rug at the front door. Gabe hated when he used the front door, tracking in snow and mud from outside, which was pretty much why Max used it.

The winter months were slow. All he had to pass the time was building his shed and irritating his brother. And the snowstorm outside was making the former impossible.

I'm thirty-six years old, he thought. *I should have more in my life.*

He looked up and found the little girl, Josie, staring at him as if he were a wild animal coming in for dinner.

He almost growled just to see what she would do.

"Hi," she said after a moment.

Max looked around for the mother bear but didn't see her. Should she see him talking to her daughter, chances were not good she'd welcome that.

He didn't blame her. Since the shooting, mothers seemed to have a sense about him.

But this little girl looked so forlorn and small sitting at the big table that he decided to risk the wrath of Mama Bear.

"Hi, again." He stepped over to her table and pulled off his gloves, taking a look at the book she had open in front of her. "Sudoku, huh?"

"Yeah." Her lip lifted in a half smile and her hair—hidden earlier under her pink hat—fell over her shoulder. Red. Like her mother's, only a bit more blond.

Max was at loose ends. It was snowing too hard to work. There were no repairs that needed to be done. No point in shoveling snow while it was still falling. Dad had left yesterday for downstate to talk to his lawyer about something. Alice was lying around with her feet up. And his brother must be checking in Josie's mother, so he wasn't around to annoy.

"I'm bored," he said, the words popping out before he'd finished thinking them.

"Me, too." Josie's sigh was long-suffering and pained.

"Yeah?" He pushed out a chair with his foot and sat. He liked kids and he especially liked kids with attitude, which Josie had in spades. "Want to hand me one of those puzzle books?"

"There's only one," she said, and tossed him a different book from the stack. "You can have this."

"A Barbie coloring book?" He opened it and grabbed a crayon from the box between them. "My favorite."

Josie smiled and bent over her book of math puzzles, but watched him carefully out of the corner of her eye.

He worked diligently on Prince Charming's military jacket.

"So?" he said, coloring over the medals pinned to the cartoon's chest, saving him the pain of the memories required to have earned those medals. "Where you from?"

Josie stopped looking at him, focused on the puzzle, running her pencil over the six she'd written until it was black. "We move around a lot."

Warning sirens wailed in Max's head.

"You sound like you're from the South."

"Texas," she said.

"Have you ever seen this much snow?"

She shook her head.

"What do you think of it?"

She wrinkled her nose and he grinned then, changing tactics, he held out his hand. "I'm Max Mitchell. I live here."

"I'm Josie G…Johnson." The sirens wailed louder. Something wasn't right. "And I think I live here, too."

He blinked. "You and your mo—"

"Josie?" Mama Bear was back and she was not happy. Max put down his crayon and turned to look at Delia standing, all her feathers ruffled, beside Gabe.

"Hi, Mama," Josie said, looking like a kid caught stealing.

"Max." Gabe stepped neatly into the fray. "I want to introduce you to Delia Johnson. She'll be our new massage therapist and spa manager."

Uh-oh.

"You're not a guest?" Max nearly cringed at his own question. He sounded angry that she wasn't a guest and maybe, somewhere, deep down in places he couldn't feel anymore, he was. He certainly didn't need feisty Josie and angry, sexy Delia around for more than a weekend.

"No," Delia said, stepping to stand next to her daughter. She placed a hand on the little girl's shoulder as if to remind everyone what the teams were. "We'll be here awhile."

Back off, her blue eyes said, and Max stood, ready to comply.

"Welcome," he said. "Both of you." He turned to leave just as the kitchen door swung open and Alice, his very pregnant sister-in-law, waddled in.

Hot on her heels was Cameron, one of Max's at-risk kids who now worked here. Formerly

Alice's assistant, these days he was more like Alice's babysitter.

"I tried to keep her in the office, like you said. But she wouldn't stay," Cameron said, looking both panicked and pissed off. Which, frankly, was a pretty standard reaction to pregnant Alice. She was prickly when she was in a good mood—pregnant she was live ammunition.

"You're supposed to be lying down," Gabe said, his eyes shooting sparks at his wife.

"I've been lying down," Alice griped. "I've been lying down so much my butt is flat. The doctor said small amounts of activity were fine as long as I took it easy."

"Are you taking it easy?"

"No," Cameron answered for her.

"Yes!" Alice amended, shooting Cameron a shut-up-or-die glare. As she turned, she caught sight of the audience and her fair cheeks blazed red. "Oops."

"Delia," Gabe said, his jaw clenched, "this is my wife. Six months' pregnant and on bed-rest orders from her doctor."

"*Modified* bed rest," Alice said with a thin-lipped smile. She held out her hand to shake Delia's and her smile became more sincere. "And we're being so careful it's ridiculous. Nice to meet you. Welcome to the inn."

"Thank you," Delia said. "I'm really looking forward to working with y'all."

Max noticed that Delia turned on the charm for Alice and Gabe, which made her reaction to him all the more pronounced. He used to have a way with people, pretty redheads included. Now, he felt tongue-tied. Lost. As though he was hidden somewhere and by the time he found the right words to say the moment was gone.

Everyone had moved on.

"This is my daughter, Josie." Delia stepped back and Josie stood to shake Alice's hand, the total picture of good manners, with no eight-year-old smirk.

"Pleasure to meet you," Josie said in her soft drawl.

She glanced at him and he rolled his eyes just to let her know he was on to her.

"I'm Cameron." Cameron stepped forward, holding out his hand like a grown-up and Max couldn't help but feel some pride. When Cameron had first arrived at the inn, he'd been sullen, angry and disrespectful. Looking at the sixteen-year-old now, he'd never guess.

"I'm going to show my wife back to her bed," Gabe said, mostly to Alice, who rolled her eyes. "Max? Can you show them to the West Suite and give them the ten-cent tour?"

Max had been about to make his silent getaway, but now all eyes were on him. Including Delia's wide blue ones.

"Sure," he finally agreed, careful not to look at Delia or Josie.

He'd spent ten years as a detective and it wasn't hard to figure out that things were not what they seemed with these two females. And Max hated that. It made his gut act up. He'd left the detective life behind and come here so that his gut could grab a rest.

He rubbed at his stomach and hoped that the beautiful Southern woman would get tired of the cold and isolation and leave. Soon.

GABE AND ALICE LEFT the room, arguing about the definition of *modified* and Delia and Josie were left alone with Max. Delia wanted to call the couple back, keep them close, because with their absence, Max Mitchell's presence became all the more disconcerting.

He waited silently, a specter at a respectful distance. Still, for every moment that passed, she grew more and more uncomfortable. She wanted to holler, *stop staring*. But he wasn't staring. He wasn't even glancing their way.

I'm losing my ever-loving mind, she thought. Maybe this time her instincts were right. Maybe he was a good guy. A nice man. Someone she could trust.

Dear God, wouldn't that be something, she thought.

Weirder things had happened.

She pressed her fingertips against the high neck of her shirt and the bruises along her neck pulsed with a sore, dull ache.

She was tired. Hungry. Obviously not thinking clearly. Max Mitchell was the least of her problems. Some food and some sleep and a new plan would clear part of this fog and doubt that Max seemed to create in her.

"If you could just show us to our room?" Delia said, making a point of not meeting his eyes. "We won't bother you for a tour. We need to unpack and clean up, right?" she asked Josie, tucking an arm around her daughter, who nodded eagerly.

"Do you have any luggage?" Max asked. "I'll grab it from your car."

"I can do it," she said, and quickly smiled to cover up the bite of her voice. The last thing she needed was Max Mitchell privy to the sad state of their garbage bag luggage. "I hate to put you out."

He looked for a moment as though he was going to argue. Then he nodded, spun on his heel and walked over to the check-in desk. He opened a drawer and pulled out a key, made a note in the old-fashioned register on top of the desk.

"Ready?" he asked, his thick black eyebrows arched over his dark eyes.

Delia nodded and Max was off, up the giant staircase that led up to the second-floor rooms. His long legs made short work of the steps and she and Josie practically had to quick march to keep up.

"Your room is back here," he said over his shoulder. "You're essentially alone in this part of the lodge."

"Where do you sleep?" Josie asked.

Delia gave her daughter a stern stare. Not only was she being rude, but they didn't need to know any more about this man. "You don't have to answer—"

"It's no problem. I'm in one of the cabins this winter," he said. "My dad usually stays in this part of the lodge, but he's away for the next week, so you've got it to yourself." He shot a quick grin at Josie over his big, wide shoulder and she grinned back.

Her daughter clearly trusted him. Liked him.

He was making an effort, Delia could tell, to put them at ease. His smile, while rusty, had a trace of his brother's charm and she found herself smiling in return.

Would it be so bad, she thought, *to have a friend right now?*

"Is your cabin like the one you're building?" Josie asked, and Delia looked down at her daughter, stunned.

"A little bit bigger."

"You guys sure got friendly." She tried to make the comment sound light. As though she didn't care, but it came out accusatory and suspicious. She'd told Josie not to talk to strangers.

"Here you go," he said, standing in front of a wide door with the words West Suite burned in script on the oak panel. He held out the key, and carefully dropped it in her hand when she reached for it.

The key was warm, hot even, from his skin. She felt a wave of heat climb her face and wash over her chest. God, she was so stupidly aware of this man she could feel his gaze on her skin like a caress before he turned to Josie. Delia, in turn, glanced at him. He was handsome. Not Gabe handsome—but really, to have two men who looked like Gabe in the same family was practically criminal. Max was rugged. Strong and powerful. And his eyes…his eyes were magnetic.

"Where's your scar?" Josie asked, and Delia nearly gasped in horror.

"Josie! That's not polite—"

"What scar?" Max asked.

"Gabe told us about the scar...right here." She lifted her thin little chin and drew a finger across the white skin of her neck. "He said pirates got you, but I don't believe him."

"You don't?"

"Josie," Delia butted in. "Gabe was kidding—"

"It was pirates," Max said, giving Delia a quick smile to indicate Josie's interest was okay. And then he tilted his face, revealing a thick band of scar tissue that went from his ear halfway to his chin along the hairline of his scruffy whiskers.

Delia bit her lip and Josie gasped.

It was bad, that scar. A reminder of something violent. Something bloody and scary. Delia was sure of it.

She wrapped her hand around Josie's shoulders, pulling her slightly closer, away from Max. They were running away from those things, from violence and injury and pain. She was trying, desperately, to leave it all behind.

That's why you can't trust your instincts, she scolded herself, panicked and light-headed from the sight of that scar and the answering throb of the scratches and bruises around her own neck.

She'd been right to doubt herself, to shove away all hints that this man was good or kind or helpful to them in any way.

He was trouble.

And she was on her own.

She quickly unlocked the door so Josie could run in and flop facedown across one of the big beds.

"Shout if you need any help," Max said politely.

"Thank you," she said, forcing herself to mean it, to not run inside and lock the door against him. "We appreciate it." From inside the room Josie squealed and Delia stepped farther into the room.

"Your daughter—"

"Isn't any of your business," she snapped over the sound of her screaming instincts.

Her words hung in the air and she felt as if she'd slapped him. The sadness, the deep melancholy she sensed in him, was visible in his eyes.

I'm sorry, she wanted to say, to eradicate the hurt she'd caused. *I'm not like this, but I'm so scared of you. I'm scared of everything.*

"Right," he said as if he'd read her mind. "It's okay." He nodded, stepped back and was gone before she could blink.

Shaken slightly by Max and her reaction to him, she shut the door behind her and gave herself a moment. Just a moment to give in to all the things she really couldn't afford. Doubt. Wishes. Hopes that she could fall asleep and everything in her life would be right again. That she wouldn't have to run from Max and their strange connection. That she was a different kind of woman.

Josie darted out of the bathroom to stand in the box of light coming in from the windows. Her hair sparkled and glittered, and her smile, unguarded and genuine, was like a pinprick to Delia's heart. Josie turned to face her and slowly, like the sun setting on the flat, barren desert she came from, the smile vanished only to be replaced by caution and worry that made Delia want to howl.

"Everything okay, Mama?" Josie asked, adult worry stamped on her young face.

The past year had aged Josie, turned her from a little girl to this changeling. Divorce was hard— Delia was proof of that. Having survived, barely, her own parents' split, she'd always sworn she wouldn't put her own children through the experience.

A promise she'd tried so hard to keep. Yet, here she was.

Delia braced herself against the door, let it hold her up when her knees wanted to buckle, while she wished, with all her heart, with every cell and granule of her self, that Josie had a different kind of mom. A better kind.

"Everything is great," Delia lied, smiling. Those divorce books told her that Josie would be susceptible to Delia's moods, so if she pretended everything was okay, Josie might start to believe it. And maybe Delia could, too. Someday.

CHAPTER THREE

DELIA STROKED Josie's hair—clean and sweet smelling—over the pillow while her little girl slept. Josie would never let her do this while awake.

She used to, of course, six months ago. Before France. Before Jared lost his mind and self-control.

Delia had thought, stupidly, that the divorce had been bad enough. But this? How could they possibly recover from what Jared was doing to them?

Josie always had been such a daddy's little girl. And really, Delia couldn't blame her—Jared had been an unbelievable father. Devoted, kind, more patient than she'd ever been, that's for sure. He'd played endless rounds of tea party and dress-up. He acted as Prince Charming for Josie a hundred times a day.

But as the years stretched on in their marriage, it seemed that the better father he became, the worse husband he became. The qualities that she had found so earth-shatteringly attractive—his confidence, his willingness to fight for what he thought was right, his loyalty to friends—became disastrous as their marriage fell apart and she was increasingly what he fought against. The security she'd thought she'd found had turned to quicksand.

That had been her problem in the end—looking for security in someone else.

It was a lesson she seemed to have to relearn nearly every day.

Despite promises to the contrary—given in the rush of make-up emotion—Jared's temper started spilling over into their relationship. He brought the pressures of his job into their home and sullied it with his uncontrollable rage.

She was never right and Jared's opinion of her, which he vocalized more and more, plummeted. Until finally he started calling her stupid. Worthless. A terrible mother.

She'd moved out at that point, filed for divorce and joint custody. Probably too late, having stuck it out for Josie's sake, but life had been okay for close to a year. Jared had been stable, their relationship civil. Then her mother got sick, alone in a shabby apartment outside of Paris.

Delia twined a lock of Josie's hair between her fingers and thought about fate. About the way the world turned out of control all the time.

For Josie the past year had been one catastrophe

after another. Culminating in this "vacation" with a mother she no longer seemed to like.

Delia had the memory of shrugging off her own mother. She'd been twelve or so and on one of her summer trips to France to visit the mother who had left them. She remembered wanting so badly to be touched by her mother but wanting to deny her at the same time. Hurt her. Wound her for leaving as she'd been wounded by the leaving.

Like mother like daughter, she thought bitterly about both connections.

Josie sighed and rolled on her side away from Delia. The little girl was exhausted. She'd barely eaten anything and had almost fallen asleep halfway through her bath.

Delia felt her own eyelids flutter, the panic and fear in her bloodstream ebbing as she relaxed.

Don't start resting yet, she told herself, shaking away the weariness that stuck to her like cobwebs. There were things she had to do before she could let down her guard. She had to deal with Jared.

Assured Josie was out cold, Delia eased off the bed and grabbed her room key, calling card and cell phone from her purse.

She felt as though she was in some bad made-for-TV movie. Running around, buying cell phones from gas stations and throwing them away, using a calling card so the number couldn't be traced. She didn't even know if any of her tactics worked.

Those bad made-for-TV movies were her only guide.

The room door opened soundlessly, easing over the wide oak-planked floor. The floorboards creaked slightly as she stepped into the hallway and crept downstairs to the dark, silent dining room.

The moon still hid behind clouds and so the light sliding out from under the kitchen door was the only illumination in the opaque, thick blackness.

She was alone.

Stepping into the darkest shadows beside the staircase, she made a quick prayer to a no-doubt-incredulous god and dialed her phone with shaking fingers.

If you want to stop running, you have to do this, she assured herself. *This is the right thing to do.*

But every instinct—survival, maternal, self-preservation—screamed for her to stop, to not make the call.

"Hello?" Jared's voice was enough to make adrenaline gush through her body, locking her muscles. Her throat closed and her heart hammered against her breastbone.

"Delia? Is that you?"

Her mouth was the Sahara Desert. "It's me."

His laughter, evil and snide, rippled down her

back. "Well, if it isn't my vacationing ex-wife. Tell me, how is South Carolina?"

Tears of panic and fear burned in her eyes and she couldn't say anything.

"Did you think I wouldn't look for you there?" he asked, so mocking and confident she wanted to reach through the phone lines and claw at his face. "Your cousin runs a shelter for idiots like you. I knew you'd go there."

"I'm not there anymore," she finally managed to say. "So who is the idiot?"

"Listen, you bitch." His voice turned mean, a physical slap across the miles separating them. "I'm doing you a huge favor right now telling people you and Josie are just on a little trip. But I'm running out of patience. All I have to do is breathe the word *kidnapping* into my good friend the district attorney's ear and this little 'vacation' of yours is over."

That galvanized her. Her spine straightened and the tears vanished. The good-old-boys' club that her ex-husband was so secure in had forced her to run, had turned a blind eye to his actions and had ruined any trust she'd had in the men she'd called friends over the years.

And she'd had enough.

What Delia knew about Jared he'd never want known. And that balanced the scales.

"You know your 'friends' might forgive a man

who beats his wife," she said, her voice low. "They might understand an officer of the law taking some bribes now and again. Hell—" she was on a roll, feeling her own power well up from the ground under her feet "—an old football star like you might be forgiven a lot of things. But all I need to do is mention your involvement with the vanload of Mexican immigrants found dead in the desert to the press and you—"

"You don't know anything," he said, but she could hear the doubt in his voice.

"The man they arrested was staying with you, Jared. Josie saw him in your house in the middle of the night. She heard you arguing. Before you turned him in you kept him hidden. In the same house as your daughter!"

His laughter cut her short. "Who is going to believe you, sweetheart? I am the Lubbock County sheriff. I play golf with the governor. She's just a little girl and you're an unstable mother who abandoned her daughter to go to France."

Anger blasted through her nervous system like an electric charge. "For six weeks, you bastard. My mother was dying and you wouldn't let Josie leave the country with me."

"Baby, you were never cut out to be a mother. And now you're proving it by dragging our little girl all over the country for nothing."

So mocking. So cocky. She wanted to go to the police right now. This minute. Just to see Jared's mug shot all over the evening news.

But she didn't know who she could trust. Where she could turn. And if something happened to her, if his evil web of golf buddies buried her and the evidence, what would happen to Josie?

What would happen to Josie if Jared truly understood what his little girl had seen?

"If I don't know anything, and Josie's just a little girl, why did you try to kill me? Why did Chris—" She nearly stuttered on the name.

"Sweetheart, Chris was doing his job. When he became one of my deputies he stopped being your friend. His loyalty is to me."

"His job shouldn't include protecting a scumbag like you, Jared."

"Well, then maybe he decided it paid better to be my friend than yours."

She pressed her forehead against the wall, wishing she could shove the memories of her friend's betrayal out of her skull. But they were burned there. Like the fingerprints and fingernail scratches around her neck that, even though they were a week and half old, didn't appear to be going away.

She'd thought she could trust Chris. The last person in her life who was on her side in the war between her and Jared. And when she'd gone to him with the information she had about Jared's involvement in the human smuggling, her old friend had set her up.

He told her she and Josie were safe staying at his cabin. He told her he would bring the chief of police and the D.A. to hear what she had to say. He held her and listened to her and that night, after she put Josie to bed, when she answered the door expecting the cavalry, Jared had stood there instead.

"The hospital in Charleston has records of what you did to me," she said. "And I have proof of those men you've been dealing with." A slight lie—she had no real proof. But her cousin had told her about private investigators whose job it was to dig up the dirt no one wanted found. If she told the right people, they could find the proof and they both knew it. "So why don't you cut the bullshit? If you didn't think what I knew could hurt you, you'd have already called out the dogs on me."

He was silent for a moment and it was so gratifying more tears bit into the back of her eyes. Victories, no matter how small and brief, were not something to be taken lightly these days.

"What do you want?"

"I want to make a deal," she said.

"Forget it. I'm not dealing with trash like you."

"Fine then. I'll call my lawyer—"

He laughed. "Please, no one in town would dare represent you."

She laid down her ace card and hoped it was enough to scare him away from them for good.

"My cousin knows people who would."

He paused for a second and Delia held her breath. Her cousin Samantha, who ran the shelter in South Carolina, had resources such as lawyers who specialized in these sorts of cases.

"You haven't talked to her about this," he finally said. "I know because I talked to her when I tracked you to that crappy shelter you took our baby to."

"I haven't talked to her yet, Jared. But I could."

She could hear him breathe, could imagine the vein in his forehead pressing against his skin. The ugliness in his soul turned his handsome face into something evil.

He was not the man she had married. He was not Josie's father. This man was a monster and she didn't understand when it had happened. When had he lost control? This all seemed like some absurd nightmare, one of his terrible practical jokes that only he thought was funny.

"You wouldn't," he said. "You're too weak. Too scared."

Once maybe that had been true. But she was Delia Dupuis. And she was her daddy's girl and tough as nails.

"Don't push me, Jared. You'd be surprised what I could do."

"I've seen what you can do, and I owe you for that." That night in the cabin she'd nearly split open his skull with a fire poker. When his grip around her throat eased, she'd pulled herself free, prepared to run, but rage and a long list of injuries for which she deserved retribution forced her to turn back to him and kick him solidly, viciously, between the legs.

He'd passed out from the pain on Chris Groames's floor and she'd grabbed her sleeping daughter and run.

She swallowed bile, hating herself and what she'd turned into when backed into a corner.

"Why haven't you talked to her, then?" he asked. "With all this proof you've got on me."

"You want Josie to see what you really are?" she asked, her voice cracking. She was doing the unthinkable, protecting him in order to protect her daughter. "You want her to be called as a witness against you? She's a little girl, Jared. It would kill her."

The line was silent for so long she allowed herself to hope that he was seeing reason.

"Jared, let us go. We can—"

"You talk to your cousin and she's dead," he growled.

Ice water like fear chilled her to the bone. Years ago, she would have said Jared, despite his temper, wasn't capable of real violence. But the last year of their marriage and whatever mess he'd gotten himself mixed up in with the smuggling of drugs and immigrants over the Mexican border had convinced her otherwise.

He was capable of anything and she had the bruises to prove it.

"Stop looking for us and I won't say anything. To anyone. Just leave us alone," she nearly begged.

"I'm happy to leave you alone. I'm happy to let you rot wherever you want to. But you're not taking my girl."

"I'm not letting you have her back."

"Tell me, does Josie even like you? You left her for six weeks, Delia. That's a hard thing for a kid to get over. You divorced her father. You're making her run all over the country. What are you telling her about this little trip of yours?"

"We're doing fine," she lied.

So many mistakes.

But she hoped keeping Jared away from Josie was the one good thing she could do as a mother, to make up for the mistakes she'd made. Even if Josie hated her for it.

"You're a criminal, Jared. You think I'm going to let her go back to you?"

"And you think I won't hunt you to ground like an animal? Josie is mine, Delia. You proved that when you walked away from her."

In the end, he was right. She'd left her little girl with a monster. A monster disguised as a devoted father.

She was suddenly tired, too weak to keep battling. Her adrenaline and nerves bottomed out and she sagged against the wall.

"Leave us alone," she breathed.

"You can't run forever, you—"

She disconnected the phone and pressed it hard to her lips until she felt her teeth. Her pulse chugged in her ears and cold sweat ran down her back. She slammed her fist against the wall, wishing it were her husband or Chris Groames.

How did I get here? she thought, hysterically.

Her fingers traced the yellow and purple bruises on her neck through the thin cotton of her sweater.

Two weeks ago she'd gotten back from France. She'd been trying hard to make amends with her daughter, to put aside the guilt she had about her mother. She'd been thinking about planting a garden behind her little house. Her own herbs and some tomatoes for Josie to pick when they were ripe.

But then the news story about the van of immigrants broke and her life changed.

This is too much, she thought, *too much for me to handle on my own.*

But she didn't have a choice. Jared made sure of that.

Her father was dead. Her mother, if she were alive, would be less than useless, having spent her whole life avoiding anything messy or ugly. And this was both.

Turning to her cousin Samantha was now totally out of the question.

Josie has me. Me and no one else.

And I have no one. The realization filled her with a despair so heavy, so all-consuming she couldn't breathe.

A rag doll without bone or muscle operating out of sheer habit and will, she turned only to realize the front door stood open, the silhouette of a man outlined in silver light watched her.

"JUST LEAVE US ALONE."

Max heard the snap of a cell phone shutting and the distinctive sound of a fist hitting the wall. He had a sickening sense of déjà vu. How many times had he seen this while on the force? How many times had a woman's voice, shaking with the same combination of fear and anger, haunted him? Echoed in his head long after the damage was done?

He turned to duck away, telling himself it was to let Delia have her privacy, but he knew the truth.

He wanted to pretend he didn't hear the emotional plea for help in her voice. Because he was a coward.

But as he stepped back into the night, her voice again cut through the darkness.

"Who's there?" she asked. She stepped into the slice of light from the open door, but the light didn't reach her face and all he could see were her fists pressed against her stomach.

"Delia, it's me. Max." He was careful. Quiet. He kept the door open so he could avoid turning on the overhead lights.

He didn't want to reveal what he knew instinctively she would want hidden. Her face, her eyes, the devils that chased her and from which she couldn't hide.

"Sorry." Her voice came out on a soft gust of relief and forced laughter. "You startled me."

He did a hell of a lot more than that but he wasn't about to push the issue.

"You okay?" he asked.

"Fine." She swallowed and opened her hands to reveal the cell phone. When she spoke again her accent was more pronounced. "Just some family problems. You know how it is."

He chuckled politely. She was telling half-truths, white lies that were inconsequential, while she hid something big.

She's probably having a fight with a boyfriend or her ex or her mother, for all I know, he thought, convincing himself he didn't need to get involved.

But then she sighed and her breath caught on a hiccup and something in the way she stood changed. She was cracking, falling apart right in front of him.

And if she did that they'd both be ruined. He was not the sort of man people should trust—that had been proved time and time again. He didn't want the burden of whatever she was about to tell him.

"Max—" she breathed. "I—"

"It's none of my business." He held his arms out to his side, a position of surrender. "Just like you said."

Her hands, alabaster in the moonlight, like white birds or handkerchiefs, clutched again briefly at her stomach then relaxed. He guessed she didn't realize how much she gave away with that gesture.

I'm sorry. The words flung themselves against his lips, but he kept his mouth shut.

He suddenly wanted to tell her that she was safe here, to at least offer her that kind of succor. But it wasn't true. Safety was an illusion.

Besides, she'd probably prickle and tell him to mind his own business.

"Okay," she breathed, her own act of surrender. Suddenly they were linked by whatever she wasn't saying and he wasn't pushing her to say. They collaborated on her pretense. "Thank you. I better get back before Josie wakes up and screams the place down.'

And just like that she was gone. Up the stairs and out of sight.

He stood still in the silence that she left behind, caught in an eddy that smelled of jasmine and fear.

Responsibility ate at him. The lingering ties that bound him to the oath he'd taken as a police officer cut off circulation to his brain and he had to fight the desire to go after her, to find out what was forcing her to the dark shadows.

He took some deep breaths. Told himself to see reason as he entered the dining room and reached over the bar to grab two beers from the fridge. He could see light under the door to the kitchen and he hoped that meant Gabe was up.

What about his responsibility to Gabe, to Alice and the Riverview? Shouldn't he say something to them, warn them of the possible danger that had been delivered to their doorstep by Delia and Josie.

He shook his head. This was what he'd been trying to avoid for the past two years. This very spot between a rock and a hard place. He wanted no responsibility toward anyone, so that he couldn't fail everyone. Again.

"Anyone home," he said when he opened the kitchen door. From his office, Gabe grunted in reply. Max opened the fridge and found two of the chocolate cakes he was after—one sunken and slightly burnt on one side adorned with a note: *Max, eat this one.*

He grabbed it, two forks, the two beers and pushed open Gabe's partially closed office door.

"Hi, Max," Gabe said, barely looking up from his keyboard as he clacked away on something.

"Cake?" Max asked, sitting in the folding chair opposite the cluttered desk and the big wall calendar behind Gabe. It didn't look good, that calendar. Through the summer and fall it had been filled with the names of guests, weddings, tour groups. So many names there had hardly been any white space beneath Gabe's color-coded guest booking system.

Now it was all white space. The Christmas holiday marked off in black at the end of the month.

"Ah…" Gabe looked over the computer screen at Max's cake. "Sure," he finally said and Max extended it and the fork.

"Are we getting any more guests?" Max asked, waving his fork at the calendar. "Or am I going to have to take another cut in pay?"

"I'm paying you?"

They smirked at each other, their way of showing brotherly love. It was pretty juvenile, but it worked for them.

"Actually—" Gabe stuck the fork in his mouth, clicked on a few more keys then grabbed his blue marker from the mug at the corner of his desk and scrawled in arrival times and names on various weekends for the next two months "—I posted the spa services this morning and we got two reservations from that. The New Year's package, once I added the complimentary massages, got three reservations. And this weekend, last minute, two women are coming from Arizona." He added the names JoBeth Andrews and Sheila Whitefeather to Friday's square.

"How long are they staying?"

"They didn't say."

"We've got a houseful of Southerners these days."

Gabe turned and reached out his fork for more of the chocolate goo. "What do you mean?"

"Delia and Josie."

"They're from Indiana."

Max shook his head. "No, they're not."

"Well, maybe not originally but that's their last address."

"Then why doesn't Delia have a winter coat?

And why is this the first time Josie has seen this much snow and—"

"Do you have a problem with Delia and Josie?" Gabe asked, leaning back in his chair.

Max could tell Gabe, right here and right now, that something was wrong. That he didn't trust Delia, that she was hiding something and that his gut said that something was real bad. Gabe would believe him and Delia and Josie would be gone by the end of the day tomorrow and Max could go back to constructing useless buildings and forgetting.

But that mix of fear and courage in her voice still resonated in him like a struck bell. The way her hands fisted at her stomach told him more than words and her bravado that she needed a safe harbor.

"No," he finally said. He couldn't be responsible for the two of them being turned out, not until he knew what was at play.

"You sure? I mean, she's a very beautiful woman…." Gabe trailed off as he reached for more cake and Max pulled it out of the way.

Gabe scowled and Max handed the cake over to him entirely. "Or—" Gabe lifted his eyebrows "—maybe you didn't happen to notice her looks."

"I noticed." It was impossible not to. She was a neon sign in a dark window. He found it hard to look away, and when he did, her image lingered, burned into his eyes. "But she has made it real clear that I make her uncomfortable."

"Did you hit on her?"

"Of course not."

"Right." Gabe nodded. "I forgot you're working on unofficial monk status."

"I'm in the middle of nowhere with my brother, my dad and my very pregnant sister-in-law. It's not that hard to be a monk."

"Daphne, from—"

"I'm not talking about this," Max told him definitively. His love life was no one's business.

"So, why do you make Delia uncomfortable?"

"I talked to her kid and it made her jumpy."

"She's pretty protective," Gabe agreed, and took a swig of his beer. "But I guess pretty, single moms have to be."

"That's the third time you've mentioned Delia's looks." Now it was Max's turn to be smug, to needle his brother. "You want me to tell Alice you've got your eye on another woman?"

"She'd never believe you," Gabe said, as assured as a man could be. He practically oozed satisfaction. Happy wafted off him like stink from garbage and his wife was the same way. When she wasn't complaining about having to lie down most of the time, or grumbling about the size of her

ankles or her butt she had "the glow." And when
Gabe walked into the room she glowed harder.

It was nice.

Nice to be around such happiness. Such nor-
mality. It gave him back a kernel of faith in
marriage and parenthood, faith the last years of his
job had ripped all away.

"You heard from Dad?" Gabe asked, taking one
last bite of cake then setting down his fork. He had
been complaining of the sympathy weight he'd
been putting on with his wife.

Max didn't have such problems so he finished
off the chocolate goo and shook his head. "It's
only been two days, Gabe. I haven't heard from
him since he left."

"It's so weird him taking off like that."

"Because Dad's been the picture of mental
health since last summer?" Max asked, not
sparing the sarcasm.

"You worried?"

"About what? That he'll tell Mom to come even
though we made it real clear we didn't want to see
her again?"

"Or that he went to see her?"

They were silent for a moment and Max
wondered if Dad would actually do that. Mom
had walked out on the three of them thirty years
ago. Just packed up and left in the middle of the

night, no note, no goodbyes, not even a hint that she was unhappy.

Then a few months ago she had contacted Dad asking to see all of them, like she had the right. Like the door she'd shut when she left would swing open because she wanted it to.

Max rubbed at his face. "He said he had to go talk to his lawyer about his life insurance. That he needed to get his things in order."

Gabe shrugged. "I don't know. It seems like a lame excuse."

"Maybe he's off having a dirty weekend—"

Gabe shot him a shut-the-hell-up look. Max smiled and drank his beer.

"You're not worried?"

"About Dad?" Gabe nodded and Max shook his head. "Nope. I don't worry, Gabe. I let you do that."

It was another reason why living here worked out for Max. He had shelter, clothes, food, company, gooey chocolate cakes and mindless work that kept him occupied—and he didn't have to worry about any of it. Gabe worried enough for both of them.

And now, with him and Alice finally having a baby after years of effort, his mother hen ways were in overdrive.

Which was another reason not to say anything about Delia.

Max stood. "Where do you want to put those two women arriving on Friday?"

"Cabin four, I think. It's the biggest, so if they want to stay, they won't feel cramped."

"All right." Max grabbed the half-eaten cake, the two forks and the empty beer bottles. "I'll go make sure it's in good shape."

"Now?" Gabe asked, looking at his watch. "It's midnight."

Max shrugged. "Why not?"

Gabe stared at him a little too long and all those questions his brother and father had been dying to ask since he got out of the hospital suddenly swirled around the room. They were never far away—the questions, concern and worry.

"I'm fine," he said, forestalling the actually uttering of the questions. No one would truly understand what was wrong. The guilt he carried that had nothing to do with a dead father and a dead kid.

"That's entirely debatable."

Max walked out without a second glance.

Everyone was entitled to their opinion.

CHAPTER FOUR

WEDNESDAY MORNING after breakfast, Josie was turning pages in her sudoku puzzle book, and Delia took a moment to melt a bit further into her chair, her belly full of the amazing eggs Florentine they'd had for breakfast.

She watched the sun shine on her daughter's hair and smiled. "You look more and more like Grandma Dupuis," she told her. "I'll have to show you some pictures of her when she was a little girl."

"Dad says I look like his mom," she said, not glancing up.

Delia nearly rolled her eyes. Jared's mother was half Native American. Josie couldn't look less like her if she were green.

"You look like both of them," Delia conceded, not arguing over the small things, as those books advised. "But mostly you look like you."

Josie peeked at her out of the corner of her eyes and smiled.

Score one for mean old Mommy, Delia thought, pleased with even that small gesture and let her bones sink deeper into the chair.

Her back hurt from the past three days of hard labor, finishing the work on the spa. It was good work—mindless and demanding—and while she painted and hung pictures and shelves, her thoughts stopped turning in constant circles.

It felt good not to think and, as she sat in the sun now, she let go of her concerns, the demons.

You've earned it, she told herself, sipping her tea. *Take a break for a second.*

Peace. She could feel it, just a few breaths away.

From the other side of the kitchen door she heard the low rumble of Max's voice and all melting in her body froze at the sound.

Three days had passed since that night in the foyer and she still burned with embarrassment and anger at herself for that moment when she'd nearly collapsed under the weight of her life and told him what was happening.

She'd nearly asked him—a stranger, a male stranger with scars and haunted eyes—for help. She'd been reminding herself of those scars, of the sadness in his eyes, but her instincts, wayward and crumbling under pressure, kept saying those things didn't matter. She could trust him.

And now, after those moments in the dark

when his low voice had stroked her, his quiet presence stirred her, her body was getting in on the conversation.

It had been so long since she had felt this kind of attraction. Slow and hot and wrong. Her speciality.

You need to be stronger than that, Delia Dupuis. Her father's drawl reached out from the past. *Where's your backbone?*

Avoiding Max was easy as he seemed to spend nearly every minute out in that clearing. So, even if she'd been looking for him or waiting for him to walk into a room or sit down to dinner—which she decidedly was not—it didn't happen. Until now, and she found herself choking on her sudden nerves. Her body going warm in places it had no business going warm.

"Saddle up, kiddo," she said to Josie, grabbing their coats from the hooks by the big front doors. "Let's go for a ride."

The look of pleasure on her daughter's face indicated this little field trip into the wilds outside of the Riverview might be long overdue.

"Where are we going?" Josie asked, shrugging on her coat as they stepped into the frigid mountain air.

"Oh, I don't know—"

Good Lord, why do people live here? she wondered, flipping her long hair out from under the collar of her coat. "Let's go into town and get some hats and gloves and stuff."

Josie stopped walking and Delia turned, waving her on, feeling the cold seep into her bones. "Come on, aren't you freezing?"

"Are we going home?" Josie asked, the wind blowing her hair back.

"Not right now," Delia said, stomping her feet to keep the circulation going. Her tennis shoes didn't offer much by the way of warmth. "We're going to—"

The expression on Josie's face was colder than the snow and ice, the air that Delia breathed.

"Are we ever going home?"

Oh, sweetie, don't ask me these questions.

She took a deep breath, the chill bracing her for the conversation. "I don't know, Josie. Don't you like it here?"

"No." Delia could see the storm clouds brewing on her little girl's face. Josie's anger was something she got from her father, quick to come and just as quick to blow over.

"Oh, come on, that's not what you said last night. Remember, you said you loved it here," she cajoled.

"You said we're on vacation, Mom," Josie said, her voice echoing against the lodge and trees. "That's what you said. This was a little trip."

"Shh." Delia approached her, wishing Josie would calm down so as to not make a scene. Josie leaped away from her. "I know I said that." Delia tried to be calm. "But I like it here and I thought maybe we could stick around awhile."

"I want to go home!" Josie cried.

"Well, we can't right now."

"Why not?"

Delia had no answer for that and Josie could tell. "You're just being mean."

With that, Josie took off running through the parking lot, no doubt heading for the trail into the forest.

Damn, Delia could practically feel eyes watching her from the windows of the inn.

Delia caught up with her daughter at the edge of the parking lot. She snagged the hood of Josie's jacket and held on tight.

"Josie, I need you to calm down."

"I want to go home! I want my daddy! Why won't you let me talk to my daddy!" she cried again, pulling away even though Delia got on her knees and wrapped her little girl in her arms.

Snow seeped through Delia's pants and her knees went numb even as regret gripped her heart.

She'd told her daughter half-truths and white lies in order to protect her from her dad's crimes. Josie didn't know that Jared had attacked Delia that night in Chris's cabin. Josie didn't know of the years of escalating emotional abuse.

Delia wondered, kneeling in the snow-filled parking lot a thousand miles from home, what was the point of keeping Jared's secrets from his daughter. Why protect him?

But she knew she wasn't protecting him. She was protecting her daughter.

And while Jared was a rat bastard and deserved jail time—and more—for his crimes, she wasn't going to put her daughter in the position she'd been after her mother left—the child keeper of an adult hate that would rob her of her father and her childhood.

Delia was stuck, hoping Jared wouldn't find them. Would maybe give up and they would never have to face a trial or the media frenzy. Her skin crawled at the thought of her daughter on the witness stand or being led, crying and scared, past a group of reporters shouting questions and accusations about Jared's criminal life.

What would be left of Josie's childhood after that? What innocence could withstand something so ugly and scary?

That was what she was trying to protect: her daughter's girlhood, her faith in her father and maybe, in a bigger sense, her faith in humanity.

"I want to go home!" Josie pushed and pushed,

trying to get away, and the more she pushed, the harder Delia held her. She'd been avoiding this moment since Josie woke up the morning after the attack, looked out the window at the Ozark Mountains and asked her what they were doing.

"Sweetheart, I need you to calm down."

"I want my daddy! Why won't you let me call him?" Josie screamed, tears running down her cheeks, and Delia felt anger flame in her stomach. Even while trying to keep her little girl safe, she was still second choice.

"Josie." Her voice was a little firmer, trying to break through Josie's meltdown before all the Mitchells walked out to witness this special maternal moment.

Just like that, Delia felt a burning heat at the back of her neck, a sense that *he* was here. As if every nerve ending was a radar seeking him out, only coming alive when he arrived.

"Everything okay?"

Delia hung her head for a brief moment, and Josie went absolutely still in her arms. Of course. Of course it would be him. Max. The silent watcher. Coming out of hiding to participate in this scene. Her skin suddenly felt hot, as though his gaze could scorch her through the sweater and coat she wore, across the distance of the parking lot and the cold air between them.

She felt touched. Burned.

"We're fine," she said over her shoulder. Max stood at the kitchen door, a steaming cup of coffee in his hand. His shirt was red and his hair looked blue-black in the sunlight.

Why him of all people? What did she do to deserve him?

Her daughter stopped fighting her then and she knew the answer. Delia had left her little girl with Jared for six weeks.

She deserved Max and her torn feelings about him and her wayward instincts and confused trust. She deserved him and more.

"Max," Josie said, her tantrum gone. She waved shyly at the man. Delia didn't look but she was sure he waved back.

She sensed him behind her awhile longer, but she didn't turn, didn't face him or engage him. She needed him gone.

Then he was. She didn't hear him or see him leave. She simply felt his absence like a cold draft sweeping across her spine.

"Sweetie," she finally said to her daughter, wiping the fine red-blond hair off her face. "Can we talk about what's bothering you? I can't help you if you don't talk to me."

Josie's chin was out, her eyes red and wet, her face mutinous.

"Please?" Delia asked, following the counsel of those books to the letter. "I don't want you to be upset or angry."

"You said we were on vacation," Josie said, squinting at her.

"We are," Delia protested, splitting hairs.

"But now you've got a job. You don't get jobs when you're on vacation."

"I know." Delia tried to hold her daughter's mittened hands, but Josie jerked them away. "But this isn't a normal vacation."

"Why can't I just go home to Dad? You can have your job here and I can live with Dad. Like before."

When you left. The words, though unsaid, practically echoed through the forest, around the buildings, stabbing Delia right in the heart.

She took a deep breath. The Daddy's-at-a-conference excuse had clearly lost its effectiveness and, while she'd tried to avoid telling Josie the truth, she couldn't concoct another lie. She didn't have it in her. "Your dad is in trouble right now, and you can't live with him."

"What trouble?"

"Remember when we were watching TV and you saw that guy who'd been arrested and you said that you'd seen him before? That he was living with Dad?"

"Yeah, Dave. Dad said he was staying with us until his apartment was ready."

"Well, your dad was working with him. Doing some really bad things."

Josie's face screwed up in petulant disbelief. "No, he wasn't! Daddy is a policeman," she said, as if Delia had never heard of the word before. "Policemen don't do bad things."

Anger exploded across Delia's nerve endings and she stood. "Well, if he didn't do bad things, why was that bad man living with you?"

"I told you he was waiting for his apartment to get ready."

Delia almost laughed, incredulously. It was so simple in Josie's world. Dad was one of the good guys. Mom, on the other hand, was questionable.

"Josie, you just have to believe me. Dad has to get some stuff straightened out about what… Dave was doing." She hated that her daughter even knew his name. That Jared would be so stupid as to let that man step into the same house as his daughter.

She recognized she left a lot to be desired as a mother, but surely on the spectrum of bad parenting, Jared's mistakes had to place him in proximity to her.

But Josie missed her father. It was written all over her face.

"But why did we have to leave?" Josie asked. "We could have stayed and helped him."

"He wanted us to go," Delia lied. "He wanted us to be safe."

Josie digested that fabrication and Delia could see it made her feel better. She breathed a silent sigh of relief.

"When can I talk to him?" she asked.

"Not yet, he'll call when he's able to talk."

I'm sorry. I'm so sorry for these lies.

"But he doesn't know where we are." Josie was growing emotional. "How will he know where to call us?"

"I have my cell phone. He knows how to get a hold of us." Delia didn't bother to tell Josie that after the conversation three nights ago she'd destroyed it. She'd have to get a new one, for use as a prop.

Delia wrapped her daughter in a hug, which she didn't return. She hadn't returned one of Delia's hugs since she'd moved out and been granted partial custody on weekends and Wednesday nights. Delia could only imagine what Jared had told Josie, what lies he'd fed their daughter so she'd love him more than Delia. And no amount of love or affection melted the ice her daughter was cloaked in.

"You understand why I had to leave, don't you?" she asked for what had to be the hundredth time. "Why I went to France?"

"Yes," Josie said, playing with the zipper on her coat. "Grandma was sick."

"I wanted you to come visit," she said, and Josie looked at her boots.

"That's not what Dad told me," she murmured. Delia, while not surprised that her husband had said such things, was surprised that Josie revealed it. Maybe there was a thaw coming after all.

"Dad got it wrong," Delia said. "I think he was mad at me and didn't want to let you come."

Josie shot her a highly dubious look that spoke all too clearly of how perfect her father still was in her eyes.

"I would like to make up for that time I was away," Delia said hopefully.

Josie's gaze practically screamed, *You're my mom, you should already know me.* But Delia wasn't sure if she projected that guilt onto her daughter. She didn't know what was real anymore. What was real and what had been fabricated by Jared. Her father. Her own fear-crazed head.

"How about if we start with a drive into Athens to get a hot chocolate?" she asked.

"With whipped cream?"

"Like there could be any other kind."

Delia held out her hand, wishing her daughter would just take it without looking at the offering as though it was a snake that might bite.

"I miss Daddy."

Delia bit her lip to keep from screaming. "I know you do," she managed to say, calm and adultlike. "How about this? Anytime you get lonesome for Daddy, you can talk about him with me."

Josie shook her head. "You don't like him."

Truer words had never been spoken. But Delia could see where Josie was going with this.

"You can't talk to Max about your dad."

Josie blinked up at Delia. "Why not?" she whispered.

"Because—" She crouched, stalling for time. *I almost spilled everything to him the other night. But I didn't and we've got to be strong. No one can be trusted.*

"Because the trouble your dad is in is secret. He could get in more trouble."

More lies. Protecting Josie. Protecting Jared.

What am I supposed to do? What is the right way here?

Slowly, Josie nodded and turned away from where Max had stood.

"Let's see what Athens has to offer. Okay?"

Josie agreed and they crossed the parking lot to the car. The crisis had been averted, but Delia knew Josie was no dummy and all the hot chocolate and white lies in the world weren't going to satisfy her much longer.

And Jared would find them sooner or later. Delia knew that, in her bones and gut and the damaged skin around her neck.

She either had to run again, or find a way to stop him.

MAX WATCHED Delia through the window in the kitchen door. Josie was having an average kid meltdown. On the other hand, Delia—while she may not be aware of it, and certainly would hate that she was displaying it—was close to something nuclear.

The desperation on her beautiful face pulled at him, tugged at his conscience. Tempted all those fine and noble characteristics about being a cop that he was trying to ignore.

The woman needed help. She needed help with her daughter and she needed help with whatever secret burden she carried on those thin straight shoulders.

I am not, he told himself, *the man for that job.*

"Whatcha looking at?"

Max turned to find his sister-in-law behind him, drinking a big glass of skim milk and looking like she carried a bowling ball under her green shirt.

"Nothing," he said, burning with embarrassment that he'd been caught watching Delia and Josie.

Of course, as he left the window Alice stepped forward to see for herself.

Nosy. Everyone here was so damn nosy. It's what he got for working with his family.

"Ah." She gazed at him over her shoulder, her dark eyes twinkling. "Gabe said you had a thing for her."

He just scowled and poured himself more coffee.

"She's pretty," Alice probed.

"She's trouble," he said, without thinking. Alice's eyebrows skyrocketed and he cursed himself. "I don't have a thing for her. I'm just saying I think she's hiding something."

Alice faced the window again. "Really? You gonna do something about it?"

"Like what?"

She shrugged as she turned to rest her hip against the counter, and stroked her hand idly over that bowling ball. "Investigate, or something."

He shook his head, nearly laughing. He was going to stay far away from Delia and her little girl.

"Where's the dad?" Alice asked then took a swig of her milk. "Has she said anything about him? Are they divorced or—"

"There have been no interrogations, Alice," he chided.

"Well, you should find out," she said with a grin. "It would be bad news to fall in love with a married woman."

He spun away before she could see all the color drain from his face. It was a lesson he'd already learned.

He screwed the cap onto his travel mug of coffee, nodded at his nosy sister-in-law then headed for quieter pastures.

"No one believes you, you know," she said as he was halfway out the door to the dining room.

He sighed, but played along because she was pregnant with his niece or nephew and he loved her. "Believes what?"

"That you're such a hard-ass. Underneath all those flinty glares and scary scars you're a softy."

His stomach squeezed tight and he found it momentarily hard to swallow. She was right. He was too soft. That was why he had left the force. Why that teenager and his father were dead. Max had let his heart make decisions when it had no business getting involved.

He glanced at Alice and she cocked her head to the window behind her, where Delia was taking Josie's hand and leading her to the car. "She might need you, Max. And maybe, you might need her."

"I don't need anything," he said, to both of them and he hit the door without looking back.

CHAPTER FIVE

DELIA SET DOWN the holistic health catalog and typed out the last of her order. She was using Gabe's computer to place the order online and since the Riverview already had an account with the company for the shampoo and soaps in all the rooms, she didn't need to worry about payment.

But the spa was empty of supplies so the delivery needed to be rushed. Today was Thursday and two older women had scheduled messages for Saturday, plus she had a couples massage on Sunday.

Delia rubbed her forehead. She and Josie could run into Albany to pick up some stopgap supplies.

She heard Josie's voice in the kitchen where she was helping Chef Tim roll out pastry dough.

Guilt and gratitude warred in Delia. These people were so kind, taking Josie under their collective wing and acting as if they had just been waiting for a little girl to come around to help. As Tim explained it, they were all practicing for Gabe and Alice's baby.

"Cameron, I swear to God, if you don't— Oh, sorry." Alice stood in the doorway, a nervous Cameron behind her.

"I'm just placing an order for the spa." Delia rolled away from the desk as if she'd just been caught embezzling. "Gabe said—"

"It's fine, Delia," Alice said. "I was just coming in here hoping to hide out." She shot a disgruntled look at Cameron, who threw his hands in the air and walked away.

"It's not like I don't have better things to do," he cried.

Alice smiled, easing into the chair across from the desk and propping her feet up on the milk crate set there for that exact purpose.

"How are you doing?" Alice asked, folding her arms over her belly. "We haven't had much chance to talk."

"I'm good," Delia said, smiling through her lies. "Excited about being here."

"Well, that's lucky, we're excited to have you here."

"It's win-win," Delia said as a joke, since they'd never know that this job was a landslide victory for her. "How are you feeling?" she asked, attempting to turn the conversation away from her.

"Like a bloated whale washed up on a shore somewhere."

Delia laughed, remembering the feeling all too well. "Well, it gets—"

"So help me if you say better, I'll poke myself in the eye with a fork. Everyone keeps saying that."

"I was going to say worse." Delia winced. "I gained so much water weight with Josie I had to wear my husband's shoes home from the hospital. I had a baby, a sore crotch and man-size feet. It's much worse than feeling like a beached whale."

Alice's pregnant belly shook with her laughs. "Oh, that's good. It's so nice to hear some honesty."

Delia's laughter sank to her feet, weighted down by new guilt.

"Well," she said, turning to leave. "I'd better—"

"Have you checked in to school for Josie? I mean, after the holiday break?"

"Yep," she lied. "We're all signed up." She'd love to sign her daughter up for school, but she didn't think they'd be here that long.

"Are you raising Josie alone?" Alice asked suddenly, and Delia blinked, stunned into temporary speechlessness. "You mentioned your husband, but you're here alone. I just wondered—" Alice shut her mouth, blushing slightly. "Sorry. I…ah…I guess I'm starved for a little conversation."

"My husband died."

The words popped out, unplanned, setting up a whole new set of lies. Of checks and balances

Delia would have to keep straight. But even as the words rolled off her tongue, it didn't feel like a lie. The man she'd married, like the person she'd been, had vanished at some point, buried under the rubble of their marriage.

It felt good to wash her hands of him at least in this small way.

"I am so sorry." Alice looked totally chagrined.

"It's okay," Delia said, making sure she sounded as though it wasn't, so Alice wouldn't ask any more questions. She'd have to tell Josie that if anyone asked her father was dead. Oh, God, she could just imagine what that would do to the poor girl, the confused hysterics the latest lie would cause.

"Delia—" Alice leaned forward and grabbed her hand, and Delia fought the urge to pull away "—I just wanted to tell you how great it is that you're here. Since we started advertising the spa services, we've gotten double the number of reservations. We were worried we would have to lay off Cameron for the winter, but now we won't have to. Which—" she tilted her head to peer through the open office door to where Cameron worked, oblivious to their conversation "—is a lifesaver."

Alice kept talking about the baby and bed rest and worrying about Gabe, but Delia couldn't hear her for the pounding of blood in her ears.

She was going to leave these people high and dry. It was inevitable. One night in the not so distant future she'd pack up her daughter and their meager belongings and—she wasn't proud to admit it—all the free shampoo and soap she could get her hands on, and she'd be gone.

All while these people were counting on her.

"I better go check on Josie," she said, interrupting rudely. "She's probably under Tim's feet." She tried to laugh, the merry tinkle of a laugh that her mother had perfected as a smoke-and-mirrors abstraction that buffered reality.

It's cancer, but what's a little cancer? Ha-ha.

I'm leaving, sweetie, but you'll love to visit me in France. Ha-ha.

But Delia could tell by Alice's face, the confusion there, that she didn't have her mother's merry way with distraction.

Regardless, she had to get out of this room. It was getting hard to breathe.

"All right," Alice said. "I'll see you at dinner."

"Great," Delia agreed, moving to the door, painfully aware that Alice watched her.

"Delia?"

She turned, her mouth too full of her lies to talk.

"Thanks." Alice lifted a shoulder. "For the honesty. It's nice to have another mom around."

"No problem," Delia said.

She had to leave. She was a fraud. And the kinder these people were to her the worse she felt.

"IT'S PRETTY, isn't it?" Iris Mitchell asked, drinking in the snowy view through the windshield of their rental car.

"If you like snow," Sheila Whitefeather muttered, yanking on her gloves and pulling her hat down over the sparse regrowth of brown fuzz on her head.

"Look." Iris ignored her friend's sarcasm and pointed out the window at a deer that lingered at the edge of the forest to their left. "It's so wild here."

"We have deer in our subdivision," Sheila countered, clearly rooted in her sarcasm. The snow and the cold, Iris knew, didn't agree with the woman's thin Navajo blood.

Iris let it go, too happy, too thrilled and filled with wonder and worry to deal with Sheila. They'd been friends a long time, which explained why Sheila was here and why Iris could ignore her right now.

She looked back at the magnificent stone and wood lodge and prayed to God—who, oddly enough, had been listening to her more lately than ever in the past—for the strength to handle what was to come. For the grace to deal with the anger that would be laid at her feet. And, if he had a moment, if he could send one of her boys out that front door so she could get a good look at Max or Gabe, well, that would be great, too.

"You worried?" Sheila asked, her hand clasping Iris's where it clutched the steering wheel in a death grip.

Iris rested her forehead against their clasped hands. "Scared to death," she confessed in a whisper.

"Okay." Sheila's matter-of-fact voice told Iris that they were going to be reasonable now. Attack this reunion as though they were mapping out an election campaign. It was Sheila's strength, meeting things head-on. Cancer. Death. Reunions between Iris, her husband and the sons she'd left behind. Sheila was strong where Iris was weak. And vice versa in so many ways.

"What's the worst thing that could happen?" Sheila asked.

"Well." Iris sighed as she straightened. "I don't think it's overly dramatic to think there might be weapons involved. I think they might throw things at me. Patrick, I'm sure, will want to strangle me."

Sheila patted her hand. "All right. We can practice ducking. But I, for one, don't think they'll even recognize you. Thirty years have gone by. The boys probably don't have a clear picture of you in their head and Patrick, no doubt, burned all the photos and—"

Not recognize me? Iris thought, pained—though she did not have the right—by such a notion.

"Okay, let's stop being reasonable," she said. Reasonable was hard. It hurt. It was something she'd never been good at.

In the years that had passed since she'd seen her family, her memories of them—the curl of Patrick's biceps, the feel of Gabe's hair under her hands in the bath, the sweet weight of Max against her when he fell asleep and she had to carry him from the car—had been bronzed, undiminished by the ever-forward movement of time. That she might be forgotten so utterly seemed ludicrous.

"This is ridiculous, isn't it?" she asked. Again.

"Yes. Completely."

"But I have to do it, right?"

"So you say. But if you need to say it again, go right ahead."

"I'm getting older. I mean, I could die tomorrow. I could get cancer—"

"It's not contagious," Sheila said with a raised eyebrow.

"I'm saying—" Iris took a deep breath, *what am I saying?* "—that life is fragile and I've pretended for thirty years that this was something I would do—later. When I was stronger. Better. And well…later might not come. I might die. Something might happen to one of them and I'd never know. It's later now and I have to do it."

"Okay." Sheila nodded as if the answer satisfied her. "What are your expectations? What do you really want from this?" Silence filled the car and Iris could only hear her own heartbeat and Sheila breathing. "Do you want forgiveness?"

In the millions of times they'd talked about this, forgiveness had been something they never discussed. The pink elephant in the middle of the room.

"That's a bit lofty, isn't it?" Iris joked to protect herself, because of course she wanted forgiveness. She wanted her boys and her husband to wrap her in their arms and tell her they understood. But that wouldn't happen. She knew that—Patrick had told her in his letters that it wouldn't happen.

She didn't deserve that.

But considering Patrick's role in her absence she figured maybe she did deserve an apology.

"I want Patrick to explain why he wouldn't let me come back. I'd told him I was better. That I found meds that were working," she said, perking up a bit, warming with this long-held resentment.

"Ah, but you didn't tell him the whole truth, did you? So, you can't put all the blame at his feet," Sheila reminded her.

Right. Yet another reason Iris wasn't allowed to

hold a grudge. Another reason she shouldn't expect or even want forgiveness.

Iris knew Patrick. If he'd known the whole story, he would have moved heaven and earth to have her back. But she would never have known if they were together again because he still loved her, because he'd forgiven her. Or if he was simply tolerating her so his family could be together. And she couldn't live like that.

"I wanted to be wanted," she said. "For me. And me alone. When he said, 'Don't come back,' I knew he didn't want me. But why wouldn't he divorce me?" she looked at Sheila, who was nodding along. The anger that Iris had tried not to feel because she had no right to it burned white-hot in the center of her reasons for being here. "If he didn't want me anymore, if I was such a curse upon his life, why are we still married? Tell me what sense does that make?"

"None."

"And did he even tell the boys that I wanted to come home? And that he told me not to? I bet not." She shook her head, gathering her hat and gloves from the console between them. This inappropriate anger put wings on her feet and suddenly she was anxious for answers. "Not my 'don't rock the boat' husband. My guess is I've been the bad guy for a long time."

"Probably."

"Well, then I think my expectation is to get an apology from my husband and to apologize to my boys. And if we can move on from that in some kind of fashion—then wonderful. And if not, I can go to my grave knowing I gave it my best shot."

"And I can go to my grave having seen more snow than should be allowed," Sheila said, her smile bright in her pale face. "Navajo don't like snow."

"Understood. I am forever in your debt." Iris nodded and looked back out the window, hoping again for a glimpse of one of her boys. But there was only a little girl exiting through the front doors, her pink jacket a bright spot in the white landscape.

Is that my granddaughter? she wondered, her gaze clinging to the girl as she stepped down a trail in the woods on the opposite side of the parking lot.

"Are you going to tell them about Jonah?" Sheila asked the other question Iris had taken great pains to avoid.

"I don't know," she answered, truthfully, shaking her head. "I thought I'd play that one by ear."

"Well, then let's go in and get this damn charade started." They both opened the doors and gasped at the cold air that swept in. "What did you tell them when you made the reservation?" Sheila asked.

"That we were lesbian lovers celebrating our anniversary," Iris said, straight-faced.

"Wonderful, my husband will love that."

It felt good to laugh, even if it was out of place in this serious moment.

They left their bags in the car and picked their way carefully over the ice and heaps of shoveled snow and finally made it to the cleared sidewalk that swept around to the front of the building.

The Riverview Inn was beautiful. Truly. It filled her with a long-gone maternal pride that the two boys she'd known had grown into the kind of men who could build something like this with their hands and the sweat of their brow.

Of course, Patrick would have helped.

Her heart stuttered and she paused for a moment. Static, noise and fluff, filled her head. Patrick. Patrick. If he was here, would he know her despite the years? Or would he simply see the silver hair that had once been black as coal? Would he look past the wrinkles in skin that had been smooth? His wife had been lean and strong where now she was soft and round. Her breasts were bigger, her belly fuller.

She knew in her bones that no matter what the years had done to Patrick she'd recognize her husband. She'd know him if he'd lost all his hair, wore glasses or even a mask.

"You coming?" Sheila asked, holding open the big front doors.

"You shouldn't be doing that," Iris chastised her friend and herself for letting Sheila do too much.

Sheila rolled her eyes, but sagged slightly when Iris took the weight of the door away.

"If you're going to treat me like I'm dying, they'll never believe we're lovers," Sheila muttered, and Iris laughed.

"If you take off your hat, they'll never believe we're lovers. I've never liked bald women," Iris joked back, but her gaze scanned the empty room searching for one of her boys. Her heart pounded so hard her ears throbbed and her chest ached.

"You okay?" Sheila asked, wrapping an arm around her waist. Iris nodded, unable to speak for the nerves. "We don't have to do this. We can—"

A door swung open, revealing a kitchen and a tall dark-haired man.

"Oh my God," Sheila breathed, and Iris's knees buckled. "He's your spitting image."

"Max." She sighed, her head swimming. Sheila held her upright.

It was her Maxwell coming through the door. Named after her father.

He caught sight of them and stopped. Blinked then smiled awkwardly and Iris knew this boy as her own. The boy that had taken after her, not just in looks but in spirit, too. Max had been moody and quiet, a foil to his blond, gregarious brother.

She prayed that her plague, the sickness she dealt with, didn't infect him as well.

"Hi," he said, a shy half-grin that managed to be both welcoming and awkward on his face. "Are you checking in?"

"Yes," Sheila said.

Oh, what did I do? What did I give up? Iris raised a trembling hand to her face, suddenly overcome with guilt and shame and a horror that she'd allowed herself to let go of her family.

What am I? she wondered, shaken to the roots of her person, ripped away from the firm moorings of who she thought she was.

"Are you okay?" he asked, approaching with his hand out as if to stop her from falling. His eyes were sharp now. Focused. She knew he'd been a cop, a good one, honored several times for bravery and courage. He'd always been a boy happiest with something to do. Something to build. Work on. A problem to fix, a puzzle to solve. "Do you need—"

"I'm fine," she said. She glanced at him, smiling, but had to look away as if he were a too-bright sun.

"Tired," Sheila filled in. "From the drive. We have reservations. This is—" She paused and Iris knew she was unsure if she'd used her real name. Such a ruse. Such a ridiculous errand coming out here.

Max spun the registry book on the desk beside

them a quarter turn and read whatever was written there.

"JoBeth and Sheila?" he asked, filling in the silence with his no-nonsense voice.

"That's us." Iris aimed for bright tones but sounded like a frog and Max's eyebrows pulled together.

"My brother usually does all this stuff." He waved his hand over the book, indicating just what he thought of those things his brother took care of and Iris almost smiled again. It was as though they were still boys. "But, I'll show you to your cabin and you can check in later after you've rested."

"That would be wonderful," Sheila said, still holding Iris around the waist. It was no longer necessary, but a comforting support all the same.

He led them out the door and down the shoveled path toward a lovely green cottage with white gingerbread trim that faced the lodge across a large open field, that was probably a garden in the spring.

Sheila asked questions about dinner times and spa services and Iris let it wash over her as she watched her boy, finding traces of Aunt Celia in the straight line of his nose, a little of her father in his smile and dark eyes. But this boy was her son. The dark hair, the high cheekbones. The full lips that curved slightly downward, indicating a serious nature that his brother and father did not have.

Just like her.

He opened the door to a lovely, sun-splashed room and turned to face them. She didn't turn away, having gotten control over herself and when he smiled at her, she smiled back. Not only her mouth, but her whole being smiled back. He blinked, and blinked again, seeming suddenly confused.

"I'm sorry." He shook his head. "Have we met?"

Iris's mouth fell open, words vanished, and her breath stalled in her throat.

Sheila stared at her. Her son stared at her and she could only open and shut her mouth, unprepared for this moment. After years of anticipating it, imagining what she would say and how it would be received, she was broadsided by the heaviness, the impact and weight of what she had to say to this man.

Oh, sweetheart, my little boy, I'm so sorry.

Sheila, God love her, stepped into the breaches of Iris's life and made them her own.

"My lover and I would like some privacy," she said, her voice echoing through the great outdoors.

Iris gulped back a startled laugh and Max's mouth fell open slightly.

No one moved. They were all paralyzed, so Sheila took off her hat, revealing her bald head covered in brown-black fuzz that screamed

Woman Recovering From Cancer, and held out her hand for the key.

Max gave it to her, inclined his head and left, silently.

"Well," Iris said, watching him go, laughter chasing pain through her bloodstream. "He'll never guess who I am now."

"Maybe it will give you some time to figure out what to say if he does," Sheila muttered, pulling her cap back over her head and walking into their cottage. "And, what to say when he asks why you left."

Iris stood on the snow-filled porch, a band of sunlight across her feet, and felt on the edge of herself. Beyond this moment there was simply the unknown. Simply darkness and empty space. A new person, a new version of herself, drifted out there waiting for the chance to be born.

She closed her eyes as the cold wind fluttered around her.

Winds of change, she thought. *Nothing will be the same after this moment.*

The alarm on her watch beeped and Iris turned it off and dug through her coat pocket for her pills. What to say to the boys she'd left behind? How to explain why Patrick hadn't wanted her to come back?

Maybe she'd let Sheila do it. As her doctor, Sheila understood Iris's mental illness better than she did.

MAX SHOOK his head.

Lesbians. He nearly laughed, wondering why they'd lie about such a thing. And they were lying—it was written all over their faces. One of them, the taller of the two but somehow appearing more fragile, seemed so familiar. He searched his memory for someplace he would have met her, but nothing surfaced.

And the other woman, Sheila, she'd clearly gone through a hard battle with chemotherapy.

But lesbians? Hardly.

He took off again for the lodge. This place was supposed to be a respite from his life as a cop. Calm. Uneventful. But between those two women, the mystery of Josie and the beautiful and terrified Delia, he felt as though he was in the middle of a bad soap opera.

At least no one was in danger of being shot, he thought as he opened the door and went inside. That was a plus.

Max rubbed his hand through his long black hair and felt the tweak of curiosity, something he'd tried to quell and squash since leaving the force.

People were puzzles and once upon a time he

liked figuring them out. Had this quartet of women walked into his life five years ago he would have made it his life's work figuring out what secrets they held.

Nothing like a bullet across the neck to change your perspective.

But the curiosity was still there, as much as he tried to get rid of it.

Approaching the kitchen, he heard his brother's and Alice's raised voices. Arguing was foreplay to those two, which was pretty funny considering how much effort his brother spent in other aspects of his life avoiding arguments and confrontation.

About as much effort as Max had spent running toward a fight.

He opened the kitchen door to his arguing family. Alice sat in the swivel office chair pulled up tight to the chopping block stacked high with cookbooks. Gabe leaned against the block, next to her, holding a book out of her reach.

Childish—Max loved it.

"Hey," he said, breaking into their argument. They shut up for a second to look at him. "Those two older women are here. They aren't checked in, but I showed them to the cabin."

"Max," Gabe groaned. "There's a system—"

Max waved him off. "One of them is clearly recovering from chemo and the other one looked like she was about to pass out. And since I didn't want to have to carry her to the cabin after she dealt with your system, I figured they could check in later."

Gabe and Alice exchanged a knowing glance.

"What?" Max barked. He didn't like knowing glances.

"That's more than you've said at one time in, like, a month," Alice said.

Max rolled his eyes.

"It's Delia," Gabe said to his wife, as if Max wasn't there. "She's got him forgetting he's trying to be a badass."

"Oh, Max." Alice looked like a snitch with some news to tell. "I did some investigating of my own. Since you're too scared."

"Uh-oh," he muttered.

"Delia's husband died. She's alone. Which is sad, but good news for you."

"Ah, my wife—" Gabe sighed sarcastically "—the picture of compassion."

"I'm just saying." Alice shrugged and then groaned. "That was awful. I'm sorry. But you could ask her out."

Max tried to pretend the news didn't affect him but it did. It explained Josie's sadness, the tension between mother and daughter, the worry and grief that sometimes clouded Delia's face. She's a widow and that was a sad thing to be.

"No one is asking anyone out," he said, and let the door swing shut behind him as he left. But on the second swing he ducked back in. "The old women are pretending to be lesbians."

"What?" Gabe laughed. "How do you know?"

"The woman recovering from cancer wears a wedding ring and the one about to faint wears a gold cross around her neck," he said, and left for good this time. He'd head out to the clearing, finish framing the roof and maybe get to work on the log finish.

Some mindless work would empty his head. Banish any curiosity he had about this lodge filled with women.

TWO HOURS LATER the back of Max's neck tingled. A little tingle. A troublesome eight-year-old-size tingle. He knew Josie was behind him, standing in the shadow of the big Douglas fir.

He ignored her for a long time, hoping she'd get cold and head back to the lodge, maybe find her mother. But the girl had an obscene amount of patience for a kid and she didn't shake.

Crap, he thought, planing a ceiling joint that had been giving him trouble all morning. It was either be mean to Josie so she'd do as her mother wished, or incur the wrath of Delia. Just the thought of that, those flashing eyes and lush lips pressed thin with agitation, made his gut knot.

I do not want to get involved.

Which left him with option one.

He set down the planer and uncurled—his lower back protesting—from his position bent over the sawhorses. Turning to the girl, he fixed her with a hard stare.

"What are you doing here?"

She shrugged.

"It's cold."

She nodded.

"Why don't you go inside and hang out with your mom or something."

She toyed with her long pink scarf.

He tried not to smile. He really did. He tried to look fierce and imposing and mean. But the kid was stubborn without saying a word. He admired the tactic.

"Well." He bit the bullet. Again. Mama Bear was going to have him for breakfast one of these days, but he couldn't be mean to this kid, not when she was so clearly lonely and sad. "If you're going to hang around, you're going to have to help."

A smile, like flash lightning in the hottest part of summer, appeared and disappeared so fast he wondered if he'd imagined it. "I don't know how to build things," she said.

"You won't be building anything. You'll be holding things. Think you can do that?"

She nodded eagerly, which spoke loud and clear to how lonely she was. She did a funny little hop and skip to meet him where he stood by the side of his shed.

"Here," he said, showing her how to hold the corner of the wood he was planing. "You have to hold tight or one of us might get hurt."

She nodded, very serious, and leaned all her weight against the two-by-four. He smiled and ducked back down to work.

"What is this?"

"Ceiling joist."

She looked up at the roofless cabin and he nudged her with the wood. "Pay attention," he said, and she bent back over the wood, applying her weight.

"Have you met everyone else here?" he asked, wondering if there was a way to pawn the bored girl off on someone else. "Alice is really nice."

Her wry glance filtered through her lashes, indicating that she was on to him.

Smart *and* stubborn. He shook his head in sympathy for Delia and wondered if she'd been like Josie as a child. His gut said she had been. His gut said she had been worse. An image of young Delia, trouble in her eyes, racing off to some disaster of her own making, warmed his chest and as soon as his subconcious put it there he shoved it away.

He had no right to any curiosity about the woman. No right thinking he knew anything about her.

"Alice is sleeping this morning," Josie answered. "But she said I could come up this afternoon and meet her cat."

"Felix? He's snobby so be careful."

"How can a cat be snobby?" She laughed.

"All cats are snobby. It's their nature. And he's French. Which makes him extra snobby."

"My grandma was French. She wasn't snobby. She was nice. She let me drink lemonade out of a champagne glass."

"Fancy," he said, digesting the small tidbit of information. "Your mom's mom?"

Josie nodded and Max rolled his eyes heavenward.

You had to make her French, too? Could you cut me a little slack?

"Have you met Cameron?" he asked. "He's a nice guy. You could probably help him bake a cake or something."

Josie's wind-whipped cheeks turned a little more pink and she didn't look up to meet his eyes.

"Great," he muttered. She had a crush on Cameron. Gawky, tall Cameron whose greatest pride in life, besides his risotto, was the ability to belch the first verse of "Happy Birthday."

"Gabe always needs help—"

"Your brother is nicer than you," she said.

It wasn't the first time, or even really the thousandth time, he'd heard that.

"Why don't you go bother him then?" he asked, glancing at her through his lashes.

"He's bothering Cameron."

Max hummed in response. "Where's your mom?"

"She's working on the spa. She told me to sit tight."

"I can see you follow directions real well."

"I got bored." She shrugged as if boredom as a rationale covered all possible sins.

"We'll start getting guests today and tomorrow. Maybe some kids will show up."

She looked hopeful and Max decided he'd call Daphne, their produce supplier, to see if her daughter could come to the inn for a few hours. She was about the same age.

"Do you like your brother?" Josie asked, out of the blue.

"Sure." He blew the shavings from the notch he'd widened. "Do you have any brothers or sisters?" It didn't seem likely, but maybe one was in boarding school or something.

She shook her head. "Mom and Dad got divorced."

He stopped sanding and watched her carefully.

They could have gotten divorced and then he died. Yes, Max reasoned, trying to keep his sudden suspicion under control. *That's it. No one is lying.*

"Sorry to hear that."

"You live with your dad?" she asked. The kid didn't miss anything.

"Yep."

"Is he nice?"

"Most of the time."

"Did your mom die?"

"You ask a lot of questions."

She shrugged again. "I'm bored."

"Nope, she's still alive somewhere."

"You don't know where?"

He shook his head. "She left when my brother and I were kids."

Her eyes, amber in the bright sunlight filtering through trees, were suddenly very old. "Were you mad at her?"

He took a deep breath, a slight twinge in his chest telling him he was still pretty mad at her. "Sure. Are you mad at your dad?" he asked, rolling the dice on what had her so rigid and sad. Sadness in little kids often manifested as anger. He'd seen it happen enough to know it was true.

"No." The word burst out of her with a thousand pounds of protective force. "I'd never be mad at my dad."

Max rocked back on his heels, stunned, not so much by her answer but by her ferocity.

"It's okay," he said, wondering how he got put into the role of grief counselor. "It's pretty normal to be mad at someone when they die—"

"Who died?" She blinked as snowflakes landed on her eyelashes. The sirens in his head launched a sudden wail.

"I thought your dad died," he said carefully.

"No," she said, confused. "He's in Texas."

Blood pounded in his ears. His heart thundered against his rib cage.

Delia lied.

Josie blushed bright red as if she'd said something she shouldn't have and went back to applying all her body weight against the wood, though it was no longer necessary.

"Does he know where you are?"

"I don't want to talk anymore," she said. Studying the wood under her gloves. "Let's just work."

Rock. Hard place. Mama Bear. Secrets.

He hated this. He wanted to put down his tool and walk away. Put as much earth and air and distance as possible between himself and the tangled web that was Delia and Josie.

But he couldn't.

This was *his* home. *His* family.

"Okay," he finally said. "We can work."

He handed her a piece of sandpaper from his pocket and got her to work on smoothing out the inside of the joist.

The balances inside of him, the ones that measured cost and benefit, justice and injustice, tipped heavily out of his favor.

He couldn't ignore this anymore.

Delia was lying to them.

The man he'd been, the man he thought had died, bleeding and brokenhearted under that frog mobile, was still inside of him. Now, after two years of silence, he was saying, *No more*.

Max had been avoiding this confrontation for too long. He should have done this the moment things didn't seem right with her. The moment he met her.

It was only a matter of time before Mama Bear came looking for her cub and when she did he had a few questions for Delia.

CHAPTER SIX

DELIA PULLED her hair out of the bun she'd had it in while organizing the supplies she and Josie had bought last night. She stepped out of the spa hallway into the dining room only to find it empty.

The sudoku puzzles they'd picked up yesterday were abandoned at the big table. The Harry Potter book they'd checked out from the library sat alone beside them.

It didn't take a detective to figure out where Josie had gone: the one place Delia had asked her to stay away from.

Max's clearing.

Delia shrugged into the warm coat she'd purchased and headed out to find her daughter and her new best friend—the quiet man with the soft voice, haunted eyes and the scar around his neck.

The man she wanted to talk to, be honest with. The man her gut said might be able to help her.

Is it any wonder he freaks me out? Any wonder she avoided him at all costs?

But with Josie ignoring all of Delia's warnings to stay away, she needed to get a handle on this situation.

Snow crunched under her tennis shoes and the cold pulled and nipped at the exposed skin of her face and hands. Ordering Josie away from Max clearly wasn't working. Delia needed a new tactic. Bribery? The only thing Josie wanted, besides going home to her father, was a dog. Delia nearly laughed, imagining that conversation.

Sweetheart, if you stay away from Max I'll give you your very own picture of a dog. Won't that be great?

She started down the path and, through the brisk air, the sweet sound of her daughter's laugh rang out like a chime. Delia nearly stopped in her tracks.

She stepped into the clearing and her breath, a smoky plume in the cold air, stopped at the sight and sound of her daughter's joy.

Josie sat on top of a small ladder, reaching the end of a tape measure toward the top of what was going to be the roof.

"I'm going to fall!" she cried, her face alight with excitement and danger.

"No, you won't. I told you," Max grumbled, staring almost right into her eyes thanks to his position on the ladder.

"Don't let go!"

"Oh, for crying out loud. If you're not going—"

"I will!" Josie laughed, either ignoring or seeing through Max's gruff demeanor. "Okay, okay, but don't let go."

Josie stood from where she was perched and reached the end of the tape to the highest part of the wooden beams. "Hurry," she cried.

Max didn't even look at the tape measure. "Ten feet," he said. She let go of the metal tab and the flexible thin metal whoosed back into its case in Max's hands.

"I did it!"

"You sure did and it only took you half the day."

He was pretending to let her measure, Delia realized, her heart melting. He was giving Josie a job he'd probably done a million times, just so she had something to do. Just so she felt important.

How can you doubt that man? Delia thought. Scars or secrets or whatever sadness he carried, it didn't matter. No man could be that thoughtful and not be worthy of trust. Of friendship or equal kindness.

She felt shabby for the way she'd avoided him. For the things she'd told herself in order to keep her instincts quiet. Those parts of her body that grew warm when she thought of him turned up the temperature even more.

Josie leaped from the ladder as though she'd

been doing it all her life and Delia allowed herself to breathe.

That girl was the girl Delia remembered. The little girl from before the divorce and before France and before Delia loaded her up in the car and drove away from Texas two weeks ago.

Delia's heart felt punched and kicked, battered and torn. She'd spent so much time, so many hours trying to coax the smallest smile, a courtesy smile, a sneer of preadolescent superiority, anything, from her little girl's mouth.

To no avail.

Five days at this inn, an hour with this man and here Josie was a kid again.

Tears burned in Delia's eyes and she wasn't even sure what she felt. Anger. Jealousy.

A relief so profound she was light-headed.

She spent most of her time scared. Scared of the past, the future, whatever lurked behind the next corner. She was scared of cops and old friends and ex-husbands and her daughter. She worried late at night that her daughter's childhood, any hope for a normal life was gone, ruined not just by Jared's lunacy, but by the divorce, by the evil things her husband whispered in his little girl's ear—much like Delia's father had done to her.

But right now, at the edge of the forest, she sent up a brief prayer of thanks that they'd stumbled their way here to the Riverview Inn and, though it had taken her five days to admit it, to this man who was able to make her daughter feel like a kid again.

Her instincts were right after all.

Max was proving himself to be one of the good guys.

It felt so good, like letting go of a deep breath. Like letting in sunshine and kindness, and her heart grew.

"Hi, guys," she said, her voice ringing through the trees and snow. Predictably, Josie's smile vanished as though it had never been there, her little mouth settling into the stern lines Delia had seen for weeks.

It hurt, but Delia pushed the sensation away, embracing her relief that her laughing, smiling daughter was still in there—just not when she was around.

"Can I help?" Delia asked, and both Josie and Max looked at her, mouths agape. "I mean, if you need it. And—" she smiled "—it sort of looks like you do." She nodded toward the half-completed little building.

The two of them eyed her suspiciously and she realized then what they thought of her. What she'd become.

I used to be fun, she wanted to say. *I used to laugh and trust people. Is it my fault that's been taken away from me?*

The silence stretched so long that she felt like a fool. Her daughter, who, before the divorce, used to beg for Delia to play with her from the moment her eyes opened in the morning to the moment they reluctantly shut at night, didn't say a word.

"I can just watch or—"

"Of course you can help," Max said.

"I don't have to if you don't want me to."

"I just said you could, didn't I?"

It was quite possibly the worst invitation ever uttered to help someone build a mysterious little building. But beggars could not be choosers.

"Great," she said, clapping her hands with an enthusiasm she was far from feeling. At least this way, Josie could spend time with this guy who made her laugh and Delia could maybe find out a little bit more about her daughter's new best friend.

But that wasn't all and she knew it. She wanted to know more about him for her own sake.

Josie simply just watched her with her amber eyes.

"Sweetheart?" Delia asked, her heart in her throat, already stung and wounded by Josie's many rejections. "Do you want me to leave?"

Josie shook her head and Delia's heart bobbed upward.

"Great," Max muttered, his forced exuberance so transparent it was laughable. "The gang's all here."

"So? What are we building?" she asked.

"A shed," Max answered, and Josie shot him a dubious look. "It is!" he insisted and Delia bit back a smile. They were a little comedy routine.

"She can help me measure," Josie said, solemnly, like a serious project manager.

"Okay," Delia said, her smile bright, her hands freezing. "Tell me where to start." She blew on her fingers, wishing she'd stopped long enough to grab her mitts.

"With these," he said, yanking off his thick yellow leather gloves and handing them out to her. "You'll get frostbite."

She stared at the gloves, at his bare hands, the calluses on his fingers, the cuts along his palm, the thumbnail with the dark spot that he must have hit with a hammer or something. Those hands said a lot about him. Much the way her husband's soft, clammy hands should have warned her the first time they gripped her wrist a little too hard.

"*You* won't?" she asked, her voice a strange croak.

He shook his head and his dark eyes bored into hers.

She tried to look away, but those eyes were magnetic and she could only blink and grip the soft leather between her hands.

Who are you? she wanted to ask. *Why do I want to trust you?*

As if she'd asked the question, his lips tightened in response to whatever he saw in her eyes. As if she'd accidentally left her secrets lying about for the taking. As if with a single look he'd gleaned some important truth from her.

"Thank you," she said, breaking eye contact.

. She slid her hands into the warmth of his gloves. They were big, loose and warm, hot even, from Max's body heat. Putting them on, placing her fingers, the delicate skin of her palms against the places his had been was unbearably intimate.

The closest thing she'd had to sex in over a year.

She flexed her hands, the fingertips of the gloves hanging off by inches, and the smell of Max, caught in the soft inner lining, teased her. He turned away and she lifted the glove to her nose to sniff wood, pine trees and something underneath it all, a spicy note of bergamot and something else—smoke and danger. Max.

"We need to talk." His tone was steel plated and her eyes flew up at the change in him. The surprising hard-edged difference in this quiet man.

"Come on, Mom," Josie said, seemingly oblivious to the adult electricity in the clearing. "We need to measure all around the roof so Max can cut the logs the right length."

Max handed Josie a piece of paper and a pencil so she could write everything down. And within moments Delia found herself on the small step-ladder, bracing her daughter and handing her the metal tab so she could measure something that had already been measured.

"What are we building, really?" Delia asked Josie. "A mini log cabin?"

"I think it's a fort," Josie said. She stuck out her tongue as she carefully wrote down her measurement then stuffed the paper in her pocket and put her pencil behind her ear, identical to Max.

"For who?"

"For Max."

Delia laughed. "Why does Max need a fort?"

Josie turned, wobbled slightly on the ladder and Delia held on tighter. "To hide," she answered solemnly. "That's what you do in forts."

Delia swallowed her astonished laughter. From the mouths of babes. "I guess you're right."

They worked in silence for a few more minutes. With each moment she grew more and more aware of him behind her. Occasionally it felt as though his gaze would brush her legs, the back of her head, and she nearly whirled around to confront him.

At one point when it felt as though her skin flushed and burned under what she was sure was his secretive regard, she whirled, only to find him carefully working, not paying any attention to her at all.

"What do you think of Max?" she whispered to Josie.

"I think he's funny."

"Funny?" She looked over her shoulder at the überserious man. "Max?"

Josie shrugged, her tongue out as she concentrated.

"Has he asked you anything about—"

"Dad?" Josie interrupted pointedly.

"Shh…." Delia turned slightly and thought she saw Max glance at them but it was momentary. "Josie, please. Remember it's important that no one know what's going on. Have you said anything to him?" She almost told her daughter that she had to pretend her father was dead, but they were having such a normal time that she didn't want to ruin it.

It was hard to tell, but it seemed Josie's wind-chapped cheeks turned slightly pinker. "Did you know his mom left him and his brother when they were kids?"

Delia blinked in stunned silence. "Did she come back?"

Josie shook her head and Delia leaned back slightly against the ladder, the wind out of her sails.

"Wow."

"Hey, Mom?"

"Yeah?"

"Why were you smelling his glove?"

Luckily, at that moment the heavy sound of a handsaw biting and clawing through the wood filled the clearing and Delia was spared having to answer.

MAX COULD SMELL Delia on the breeze—shampoo, soap, gum and something else, something warm and secretive—and it was throwing him off his course.

He should have confronted her when she arrived in the clearing. He could have easily sent Josie away and gotten right to business. But Delia had looked so heartbroken, so lonely for her daughter, so eager for a chance to do something normal that he'd let his objective go. Again.

He'd made the path of least resistance his home the past two years and it was tough getting off it.

But Joe was right—once a cop, always a cop, no matter if you were a bad one. And Max's instincts, honed by years on the force, honed by domestic-crime task forces, said there was a crime being committed right now. Right here in his clearing. Too close to where his niece or nephew was curled, chin to knee, waiting to be born.

He had to do something about it. Now.

He'd given Josie and Delia the chance to talk, the chance to do something besides be worried.

They'd let the opportunity to come clean pass so now he had some questions.

"Hey, Josie," he called, putting down his tools. "I need you to do me a favor."

The mother and daughter both turned to him with their similarly shaped eyes, their red hair like bright flags in the snowscape behind them.

"What?" Josie asked, clambering off the ladder and ignoring her mother's attempts to help her.

"I'm starving. Are you hungry?" He barely waited for Josie's nod before making his request. "Can you go ask Cameron to make us a few sandwiches?"

"We just had breakfast," Delia said, and he nearly rolled his eyes. Was it any wonder her daughter resented her if she was going to be such a constant killjoy?

"This work builds up an appetite," he said, and Josie nodded emphatically. He wondered how much of his solitude would be gone for good after befriending the little girl. How much of this life he'd carefully crafted and protected with silence and indifference and a cool heart would be destroyed?

"We're going to need two turkey sandwiches. And tell him to use the good cheese, not that soy garbage that Alice is trying to get rid of. No tomatoes."

"Josie loves tomatoes," Delia chimed in, but Josie shook her head.

"No, I don't."

Max nearly winced on Delia's behalf. Instead he asked her if she wanted one.

"Sure," she said, and shrugged.

"Great, three Cameron turkey deluxes. Go. Go." He shooed Josie off as if those sandwiches were the only thing between them and immediate starvation. She took off, a pink streak through the trees.

"And cookies!" he yelled after her.

"Okay!" she yelled back, her little voice echoing into silence in the clearing.

He and Delia eyed each other across a ten-foot separation, sizing each other up. She was stunning, her white skin flushed, her red hair speckled with snow.

He'd interrogated beautiful women. Women whose gorgeous faces and perfect bodies hid hearts of such blackness it kept him up nights pacing for the children who suffered such mothers.

But this woman…her heart was not black. Her heart was right there on her sleeve and it bled red for her little girl.

Sadly, that fact didn't make whatever she'd done, or was doing, right.

"I have some questions," he said. "And things would be a whole lot easier for you if you gave me some honest answers."

CHAPTER SEVEN

"QUESTIONS?" Delia asked, stiffening with the stony fear that he'd seen a million times in witnesses terrified to confess what they knew.

"What are you hiding?" He jumped right in with both feet. Delia's eyes, blue like distant water, like the horizon where the Hudson met the sky, widened in shock.

"Hiding? What are you talking about?" She crossed her arms over her chest. Like nervous birds her eyes never landed anywhere long and her hands, wearing his baggy gloves, had a death grip on her arms. Her heart beat hard at the pulse point in her neck.

Max wanted to tell her that if she was going to lie, she shouldn't give herself away with her body language. And suddenly he was so weary. Weary of this bait and catch, this bullying dance.

"Please," he said, surprising himself. "Just tell me the truth."

She hesitated before throwing back her hair. "I don't know what you mean."

"Yes, you do. Do both of us a favor and tell me what's going on. It's obvious you and your daughter are hiding something."

"What has Josie said?" Delia asked, too fast.

"She's said she misses her father."

Delia blanched and turned to hide it. "She's just a little girl. She's—"

"Very smart," he interjected.

Delia looked over at the building, the skeleton roof. "She said you're building a fort so you can hide," she said.

"It's a shed," he muttered, but she looked at him over her shoulder and his gut tightened at the picture she made. Her beauty and foolish bravery. He just wanted to help, for crying out loud.

"What are *you* hiding?" she asked.

"Don't change the subject."

"Is this an interrogation?" she asked, bristling all over. "Are you a cop?"

Somehow she made being a cop sound a scarce step up from being sewer sludge. His gut instructed him to lie. "No. I'm not a cop and this isn't an interrogation. These are the questions my brother is too trusting to have asked."

"He already gave me the job, Max."

"And I can just as easily have him take it away,

Delia." He could and he would and she knew it. And they both knew that whatever she was hiding was making her desperate enough to need to be here.

"Fine," she said, sending out sparks into the dangerous air between them. "Ask your damn questions."

"I don't want to fight you, Delia."

"Well," she said, and tilted her chin, her eyes snapping, "you're going to have to. I'm not in the habit of spilling my secrets to men with scars on their necks who blackmail me with my job."

Their breath curled around them in gusts from their parted lips. The air between them grew warmer, the threat of explosion more definite. He stood too close to her and knew he should step away. But she was a fire on a cold night, and he was frozen to the bone.

"Your husband?" he said.

"What about him?"

"You told Alice he was dead."

"Gossiping about the bereaved? That's not a very neighborly thing—"

"Josie told me you were divorced."

"We were. Then he died. Terrible accid—"

"Josie said he's still alive."

Her nostrils flared with her sharp intake of breath.

"No more lies, Delia. Please."

Finally, her eyes shut on a whispered curse, the

fight visibly ebbing from her body. She accepted the inevitable. She'd tell him everything, but the victory was expensive and Delia was the one paying.

"Which is it, Delia?" he asked, pushing harder.

She sighed and angled her head back to look up at the sky.

"He's alive."

Her throat, delicate and white, arched. Above the edge of her turtleneck he saw the yellow edge of a bruise and an angry red scratch.

The puzzle came together with that bruise. Her fear, her worry, her fragile control.

That old rage he felt, on behalf of the bullied and brutalized, rushed his chest, pumped adrenaline into his bloodstream and he wanted to fight. Take whoever had done that to Delia and pound him into dust.

Max fisted his hands and forced himself under control.

"Why did you lie?"

Her lips parted and he could tell the words were there, right on the edge of her tongue. Against every scrap of better sense and self-preservation, he wanted so badly to touch her. To stroke her cheek, ease his hands into her hair, cradle her head against his chest and press his lips to those bruises.

To ease part of her burden, to restore some of her foolish courage and feisty attitude.

"He hurt you?" He posed it as a question when the silence became so heavy they were sure to crumple under it. He wanted to make this easier for her. For both of them. "Delia?"

Again her hands went to her neck. She tucked her fingers under the high collar of her red shirt, as if she were about to pull it down and show him. But she didn't. She stood, so still she was like wax.

"Can I see?" he whispered. "Your neck. The bruises—" When she jerked away from him, he said, "I won't hurt you. Not like him. I'd never do that."

Her gorgeous eyes filled with tears and a sudden hot rage and, instead of letting him touch her, she pulled down the collar herself.

The fading bruises and crimson scratches that could only be made by fingernails made a gory necklace.

Ah, Delia. I'm so sorry, he thought tenderly, at complete odds with the blast of fury through his nervous system. His knees nearly buckled from the onslaught of emotion.

God, he'd worked so hard not to feel anything and now this wild surge of anger and sympathy hurt.

He shook it off, tried to anyway, focused on his reality—the cold snow, his numb fingers.

But she was right there and he couldn't look away. They stood even closer now, closer probably than she realized and he could see the black flecks in her blue eyes, the shaking of her hands, the tremble of her lips. The emotions intensified, the rage and the weak knees. It was wrong in the worst possible way that this woman would be hurt by a man she trusted—that any woman would be hurt that way. But she was so strong and so scared. His hands itched to brush the hair off her forehead, to ease some of the burden she carried, to stroke away the lines of worry on her perfect face.

"Did he hurt Josie, too?"

"No." She shook her head, letting go of her collar so it could cover the marks of her husband's abuse. "He never touched her and she doesn't know about this.'

"What do you mean?"

"I mean, the—" she lifted her hand to her throat "—physical abuse was a one-time deal. He had never hit me before. Never…" She trailed off.

"Delia—"

"My ex-husband tried to kill me." The words gushed out of her as if she'd plucked her fingers from the holes in the dam. "My daughter doesn't know because it would devastate her and she's already been through so much."

He rocked back on his heels, stunned at the cosmos's sense of humor. This. Again. Another woman trying to protect her child by keeping the truth from her. He supposed in reality it wasn't that rare—most abused women probably had that instinct—but, damn, did he have to be attracted to every one he met?

"She's a smart girl, she probably realizes more than you think."

Her laugh was sad this time and again he had to clench his hands together to keep from reaching for her. "Josie believes the best of her father. She wouldn't believe me even if I told her."

"If you showed her those bruises—"

Her eyes again burned with rage, but this time he felt it directed toward him. "I won't do that to my daughter. I won't hurt her that way, put her in the middle."

"It seems your husband did that for you," he said, but he could tell she didn't see reason about this. Her mind was made up, like so many women who thought protecting their child's world was more important than protecting themselves.

"Have you at least seen a doctor?"

She nodded, zipped her coat up high on her neck. "No permanent damage."

"What about the authorities?"

"What authorities?" She practically sneered and he nearly stepped back to avoid being scorched by her eyes.

"Police or—"

"They've been contacted. They know all about it."

"And?"

"And it makes no difference."

"You just said he tried to kill you, Delia. That's attempted murder!" He was throwing himself out of his self-imposed cage without even looking down to see what hole he'd be falling into. He wanted to fight. He wanted to fight with her. With her ex-husband. With everyone.

"The authorities know."

"Where?"

"Where what?"

"The authorities where? I mean, is he in jail? Is there a hearing?"

She shook her head. "Forget it, Max. I didn't want to tell anyone about this, because I don't need you to get involved."

"Well, clearly I'm involved now. Everyone you've lied to is involved."

"Max, stop."

"Delia, there are laws to protect you. Police officers to protect you—"

"Police officers protect themselves," she spit, and her anger fueled his. Cops weren't perfect—he knew that better than anyone—but they were there for a reason.

"That's not always true."

"It is where I'm from."

"You're not there anymore," he shouted, incredulous.

"And the world isn't all that different here, I'm sure."

"There are people who could help you."

Me, he wanted to say. *I can help you. I want to.* The words clawed their way up his throat but he swallowed them.

"I'm doing fine."

"Right. Clearly. You're totally fine."

"Max."

She touched his arm and his mind went blank. His body utterly still. Even his blood stopped moving.

They panted, as though they'd been chasing each other. Connected by their twining breath and her hand on his arm and the never-ending desire he had to touch her.

As if she had read the desire in his eyes, or tasted it on his breath, a spark flared in her own eyes and he knew she was trying to control herself, too. Suddenly the air between them was kerosene and they both held matches.

Finally, she blinked and looked away and his brain started working again.

"Please," she murmured. "I…I want to forget about it. About all of it. Josie and I are here for a fresh start."

He felt the weight of her touch through the

gloves and his jacket and he longed to strip her hand bare, to hold her fingers against the heat of his body. To try in some way to repair the damage that had been done to her.

The thought chilled him, threw a bucket of cold water on his hot flesh. He'd been down this road before. Disaster waited for him should he do what he wanted.

But, right now, his rational mind wasn't in charge. His lungs burned with every breath and she didn't move her hand and that made everything worse.

Step away, he told himself. *Walk. Now. You know better than this.*

But he didn't.

"I know I haven't been very nice." She sighed, smiled and he nearly groaned from her beauty and courage. "But I want to say thanks. For Josie."

Mama Bear while angry was something to behold, but Delia with a smile and sad, grateful eyes was a punch in the belly. He couldn't breathe. He wanted to do stupid, foolish things. He wanted to lower his head, rest his mouth against hers, indulge himself in her smell and fire.

He hadn't looked twice at a woman since the shooting. He couldn't look at a woman and not see the mistakes he'd made. But this woman pulled him out of comfort and blissful uncaring.

"She's a good kid," he murmured, his whole

body held motionless by her eyes. By his stupid desire to kiss her.

"Max?"

"Yes?"

They were nearly whispering, like lovers in bed on a Sunday morning. How the clearing had become so small, so intimate, so fast was a trick he'd never understand. But he wasn't in the mood to question it. He was in the mood to whisper into this impossible woman's ear. Let his hands—

"Where did you get the scar, really?"

The clearing cracked wide open and he leaned away from her, the heat between them going stone-cold. *Good,* he thought. *Just what I needed to smack some sense into my head.*

He shook off her arm and turned to his tools, dusting off the snow that had gathered while they talked.

"Max?" She touched his jacket and he shrugged her away.

"Don't do this."

"Do what?"

"Damn it, Max! I just practically gave you my holy confession," she said. "It seems like the least you could do is answer a few of my questions."

He didn't answer. Not this question. Not ever. If she hadn't read the newspaper articles, he wasn't about to give her the abridged notes.

"It looks like a wound."

He started packing up his tools, slipping them into their cases and well-worn cloth sacks.

"Were you burned?"

He didn't answer.

"Strangled? Did your brother try to kill you in your sleep?"

He didn't answer.

"That last one was a joke," she murmured.

"Very funny."

"Max, you are a stranger to me and yet you're hanging out with my daughter. You have a scar on your neck, for crying out loud, I think I need to—"

"A teenage kid picked up a gun and killed his father and was about to kill his mother. I happened to be there. I happened—" He stopped and her jaw fell open. "I was there."

It was almost as if he could hear the snow fall and land carefully on her hair. That's how silent it was. How utterly still.

"I'm sorry," she whispered, her voice scratchy and soft. It ran over his sensitized skin like a caress.

"It's hardly your fault." He couldn't look at her just now, the words he'd never said still echoing in his head like gunfire. He continued to focus on his tools, wishing she'd leave. That she'd never come here.

"Max."

He ignored her. Needed to. Should have all along.

She touched him, and the threat of violence that had hung in the air filled his lungs and head. He whirled and did what he'd been longing to do all along.

He slid his hand into the silk of her hair, brushed his thumb against her lips and felt the caress of her startled breath.

She didn't pull away.

"Go," he said, his fingers tangled in the strands of her fiery hair. "Leave."

She shook her head. "I'm not scared of you. You can try to frighten me, but I know bad men and you're not a bad man."

His hand had moved the collar of her shirt, revealing the yellowing bruise. He didn't want to think of her hurt. Scared. He didn't want to think of her at all.

But he pulled her closer, pressed his lips to her neck and whispered, "You don't know me at all," against her tender bruised skin.

"Mom!" Josie yelled, running into the clearing, carrying a brown paper bag. "Max! I got sandwiches."

He stepped away as if he'd never touched her, as if he wasn't made of ice, dying for her heat.

Forcing himself back to stowing his tools, he put his mind in order so he could cultivate his lonely life, his only way of surviving the kind of man he'd been.

"I've got hot chocolate, too!" Josie said, her voice high with excitement. "Cameron was making sugar cookies but he said we couldn't have them. Too bad, because they looked good."

He let the little girl's chatter wash over him until it turned to white noise, the sound of static, wind. Nothing. He forced himself to think of that frog, of Nell screaming for her son to stop, to put down the gun before someone got hurt.

Max forced himself right back in the middle of that fatal situation—with the wrong feelings for the wrong woman, bleeding to death from his own blindness.

But something prevented him from getting sucked into his own personal hell again. Something in this clearing, in the here and now, caught and held him and he couldn't shake it.

Josie said that her father was in Texas.

Maybe it was time to ask Sheriff Joe McGinty to do some digging around the NCIC, to see what was being reported out of Texas these days.

DELIA SMILED and stroked her daughter's braid. "It's so good," she agreed, biting into the sandwich that tasted like sawdust.

"I know. And the hot chocolate is really good,

too. Better than in town." Josie took another big sip from the thermos, leaving a chocolate mustache across her upper lip.

Delia smiled and wiped it off with her bare hand. She'd ripped off the gloves, feeling as if they were his hands on hers. His touch burning her palms.

What the hell had happened? she wondered, panicked and freaked-out and shaking inside from the push-pull in her body.

Everywhere he touched seemed to glow as if pulsing with its own electricity. Her hand. Her lips. Her neck.

You don't scare me, she'd said, like some kind of action-movie actress. He scared the bejesus out of her.

He'd been shot, for crying out loud. In his neck! Who did that happen to?

And she wanted to think he was a good man? He was right. She didn't know anything about him, except what her instincts kept insisting. Her current situation was a pretty good indicator of how flawed those instincts were.

Frantically she tried to piece together the conversation, what she might have said. But her memory was wiped clean by the look in his eyes, the feel of his arm under her hand. His lips against her neck.

What a mess.

She hadn't said Jared was a police officer.

Neither had she said that he didn't know where they were. She'd said he'd hurt her, but not Josie. That was true. That was okay. It felt good to say that. To let that out. She felt as if she could breathe again, as if the pressure had been relieved enough so that her head stopped spinning.

Maybe it was enough and Max wouldn't ask any more questions. Max and Alice and Gabe would let her and Josie do what they needed to do, and when she had to leave, maybe they'd simply think she was a flake.

"This is a good place, Mom," Josie said and Delia nearly choked on her sandwich. It was a good place and her gut still believed that the man working and pretending they weren't there was a good man. But none of it mattered. Not unless Delia did something to make Jared leave them alone.

"I just wish Dad was here," Josie said. "Then it would be perfect."

Delia put down her sandwich, no longer interested in pretending to be hungry.

CHAPTER EIGHT

IRIS HID all day. She was a coward—that trait had gotten her into this mess in the first place.

But as she and Sheila walked up the path to the lodge for dinner, she felt pulled, compelled and eager for this reckoning—if that was what was going to happen.

Her stomach growled and she had to admit if there was no reckoning, only food, that would be okay, too.

"So?" Sheila asked. "Have you figured out what you're going to say?"

"I thought I'd see if they recognize me." Iris tucked her hands into the pockets of the old down coat that had traveled to Arizona from New York and back again.

"And if they don't?"

"Then I'll go with the flow."

Sheila stopped and tugged on Iris's arm. "Did you take extra meds?"

Iris smiled and shook her head. She couldn't actually explain this new Zen attitude, either—not after hiding all day. But she was calm and ready to walk through those doors. Like a bride going down the aisle or an inmate walking to her death—either way there was an end in sight and that filled Iris with a lovely sense of…right.

"What does Gabe look like again?' Sheila asked, tucking her arm through Iris's.

"Well, if he still takes after his father, he's got blue eyes. Cornflower rather than indigo. He's blond, or used to be anyway, white-blond, like a Scandinavian baby. He was always tall for his age, I imagine he'd be a tall adult."

Iris kept her eyes on the ground, careful of ice and Sheila's fragile bones.

"Well then," Sheila whispered in her ear, "see for yourself."

Iris's head bobbed up as if it was spring loaded. There at the top of the lodge's staircase was her oldest son. Her firstborn.

"Hi!" he said, chafing his hands together and hopping lightly down the stairs. "You must be JoBeth and Sheila."

It was like looking at Patrick the year she left and her heart sputtered and chugged at the image he made in his red sweater with his blond hair and blue eyes.

The twinkle in his eyes, the dimple at the corner of his mouth, even the silver at his temples. He was and had always been his father's son.

"Yes," she smiled, blinking back sudden tears. "And you must be Gabe."

He nodded and tucked her hand under his arm, and she couldn't help but squeeze the thick wool of his sweater in her fingers.

Hello, baby, she wanted to say. *It's me. It's your mama.*

"Glad to see you are feeling better," he said with a grin toward Sheila.

"Right as rain," Sheila said, "and starving."

Are you still stubborn? Do you still like to have your forehead stroked when you're tired? Do you still love carrots, and windy days and sleeping with your socks on? Are you still scared of heights and snakes and your brother when he gets mad?

"I'm glad to hear it. My pregnant wife has dictated the menu—"

"You're going to have a baby?" Iris asked, unable to step forward or disengage her hand from the sudden grip she'd taken on his arm.

"I am," Gabe said, looking every bit the proud father. But slowly, as she gaped at him like an idiot, that look faded back into concern. "Are you sure you're all right?"

"She's fine," Sheila butted in. "She's just found out recently that she's going to be a grandmother."

"Well, congratulations all the way around." Gabe laughed and opened wide the doors to the dining room.

Sheila pushed Iris into motion and she lurched, ungracefully, into the pretty, spacious dining room.

A grandmother.

The world tipped and swam and she wiped her watery eyes with the shoulder of her old coat.

I'm going to be a grandmother.

And the thought filled her with a joy so complete she stopped Gabe. "Children are a blessing," she told him, staring right into the blue eyes that had not changed so much from when he was a baby. Her baby. "No matter what."

"Yes." He nodded. "They certainly are."

"Hey!" A pregnant woman called when they arrived. "Welcome to the Riverview Inn. Please sit down. Max. Come on. Let's sit."

"That's my wife, Alice. We told her she couldn't eat until everyone was here," Gabe whispered in Iris's ear. "Mostly we do it because it's funny."

"Where are Delia and Josie?" Alice asked.

"We're right here." A stunning petite redhead came out of the kitchen with a young girl in tow.

They selected seats on the other end of the table from where Max sat. "Tim's finishing dinner. He says it will be two minutes."

"Wonderful," Alice said, spreading her arms. "Let's eat."

Max stood, a twinkle in his black eyes. "I think I forgot something. If you could just wait—"

Iris smiled, her prankster son still a prankster. How perfect and bittersweet.

"Leave and I'll stab you myself, Max," Alice snapped, her veneer of cheer wearing thin, and everyone laughed. Except Alice, who told them all they were going to be punished for keeping a pregnant woman from eating.

"There are no guests yet, besides you," Gabe said. "So it's just us."

"Your family?" Iris asked. She shrugged out of her jacket and Gabe hung it up on the hook, before taking Sheila's coat.

He nodded, grinning. "Such as it is, yes."

They sat at the table, Sheila next to Max and Iris next to the little girl who introduced herself as Josie.

She searched the room but there was no sign of Patrick. Relief and disappointment warred in her chest. A respite—to watch her boys.

"You and your brother," Iris asked, turning to Gabe, watching as he kissed his wife's neck and sat beside her. "You work here alone?"

"Nope, my father is usually with us, too," Gabe answered.

"Where is he?" she asked.

"He's taking care of some business downstate, but he'll be back sometime on Saturday."

Saturday. Tomorrow.

She forced herself to not ask when, exactly he would return and end this little charade of hers. Then the heartache would start in earnest.

The chef arrived at the door carrying a big bowl of spaghetti and meatballs. Alice clapped her hands and everyone got down to the business of eating.

Iris tried to imagine what might happen when her husband saw her again after more than thirty years. But she couldn't get her head around it. She doubted there would be open arms, but his last letter did say to come. Granted that was a few months ago, but—

"Do you have a phone in your cabin?" Josie, at her elbow, whispered, while her mom talked to Alice about pregnancy cravings.

"A phone?" Iris asked, leaning down to hear the whispering girl. "Of course."

"We don't have one in our room," she said. "My mom said it was broken."

"That's too bad." She tilted her head. "Do you have someone you want to call?"

"Honey?" Josie's mother asked. She had

paused in the act of dishing up pasta. "One meatball or two?"

"Two," Josie answered, and the subject of phones seemed to be forgotten.

"So, Sheila, JoBeth, what brings you to the hinterlands from Arizona?" Alice asked, happier with food in front of her. She was a radiant pregnant woman. Glowing and flushed. She appeared healthy, unlike Iris during pregnancy. She'd been sick and wasted with bone-deep tiredness and nausea.

"The snow. We love it. Especially Sheila," she answered, spooning pasta onto her plate and ignoring her friend's scowl. "How are you doing in this weather?" she asked Alice. "I was pregnant with all—" she caught herself on the word *boys* "—my children during winter. I found it very hard."

"Not too bad." Alice shrugged. "I'm getting a little cabin fever."

"A little?" Gabe asked, rolling his eyes.

"Okay, I'm going totally bananas being locked up indoors all the time." She grinned at her husband, but her voice had a certain bite that any pregnant woman would recognize. "Does that sound more accurate?"

Iris remembered that feeling all too well. Cabin fever. Such an innocuous term for what it turned into.

It had started innocently enough—a long winter with her first pregnancy. A terrible first trimester that turned into a worse second trimester. The joy everyone told her she should be feeling had been utterly absent. Instead she felt like a woman in a fog. Tired and sad and worried. Scared. And then the baby came and it got worse. She couldn't sleep at night in fear of the baby not breathing. And just when she finally calmed and the pressure eased she got pregnant again and it started all over.

Terrible. Worse. She went to visit her mother for two weeks, leaving Patrick alone with the babies. She told her mother she wished she were a bird that could fly away from what she was feeling. Eventually, like storm clouds, the fog passed and years went by.

Then Patrick took a job two counties away and that harsh winter had turned into a wet spring. Gabe had had colds constantly and Max got chicken pox and she couldn't take them outside.

Cabin fever turned into feeling trapped, turned into feeling buried alive.

And she couldn't get out of bed. She couldn't stop crying. She couldn't stop wishing she were dead.

"You have to get out," she said, perhaps too stridently, judging by the way everyone's eyes snapped toward her. "You have to take care of yourself. Make sure you have help." She turned to Gabe. "You have to help her. She can't do it all alone."

Sheila's hand on her knee, her nails digging into her skin, finally registered and she shut her mouth. Too late.

"I'm okay," Alice said softly into the silence. "I get out and Gabe is very involved."

"Of course," Iris said. Panic gripped her throat and she felt as though she were panting. She couldn't get her breath. "You're right. I'm sorry. I have no—"

"Relax," Sheila whispered into her ear. "It's okay. Take a deep breath."

"I'm very sorry," she said, when she could finally get enough air. "I just had—"

"Bad pregnancies?" Alice asked, her eyes glued to Iris's, and it was as if no one else was in the room.

She nodded. "And after," she said, through the lump in her throat. "Postpartum depression. Though at the time they didn't diagnose it so easily."

"Me, too," Delia said, and Iris looked at her. "For a year after Josie was born. It's very hard. You don't have to be embarrassed. I was on anti-anxiety meds for years. I wish I had some now," she tried to joke to lighten the mood. But Iris, who was chained to her life by antianxiety medication, couldn't laugh about it.

"Nothing is going to happen to Alice," Gabe said, his chin out, his eyes hard. "She's got lots of help here. She doesn't need to go anywhere. And scaring her isn't going to help her."

"It's not scaring me, Gabe," Alice said, putting her hand on Gabe's arm. "Postpartum depression is a reality and we should probably talk about. I know my mother didn't have it, but we don't know about your mother—"

"Alice," Max said, his voice quiet.

"Well, come on, we have to—"

"I'm going to help Tim bring out the salad," Gabe said, rising from the table.

He left a vacuum behind him and Iris felt as though her head might pop. "I'm sorry," she said. "I don't know you, I have no business—"

"It's okay," Alice assured her. "My husband just has…issues." That was all she said, but Iris filled in the blanks. Her boy had issues because his mother had walked out in the middle of the night when he was eight years old. She had walked out and she had never come back.

"Who doesn't?" Sheila said, her voice fierce in a way that Iris knew she was supposed to take to heart. It was supposed to bolster her suddenly drowning spirits.

"Amen," Max said. He wiped his mouth with his napkin then stood, towering over all of them.

"If you'll excuse me I need to run into town before we get all that snow we're supposed to."

Josie, Iris noticed, beamed up at the man but her mother, Delia, flushed and cut her meatball into careful, minuscule bites.

Issues. It seemed they had a tableful of them.

Max left and Tim and Gabe reappeared with a tossed salad that Iris didn't have an appetite for. Everyone else ate, discussing the snowstorm expected tomorrow and Iris wished she could turn back time—ten minutes or thirty years—and do it all over again, only right this time.

"I'm sorry," Gabe said to her, startling her from her careful study of her plate. "I'm a first-time father with a lot of fears. I didn't mean to jump on you like that."

So charming. So gracious. But she could tell that if she weren't a paying guest—a woman he'd have to see at this same table meal after meal until she left—he wouldn't apologize.

He could hold a grudge as well as his father.

The evidence was right there in the charming smile that didn't reach his cold eyes.

"I'm sorry, too."

For so much. For everything.

"Josie?" Delia called, and Iris turned to see the seat beside her empty. "Did you see Josie leave?"

The pretty woman's face was hard, scared, her blue eyes frantic.

"No," she answered, and everyone craned their necks to look around the room.

"She's probably in the kitchen," Alice said.

"Probably," Delia said, obviously not believing it. The scrape of her chair as she stood was like nails on a chalkboard.

"She was asking me if the phone in my cottage worked," Iris told Delia and the sudden tension in the woman hit Iris like a tidal wave. "There was someone she wanted to call."

CHAPTER NINE

JOSIE WASN'T in the older women's cottage. She wasn't trying to use the broken cell phone in their rooms. The kitchen was empty.

Delia wanted to scream. She wanted to fist her hands in her hair and howl at the moon. Josie had gone looking for a phone, Delia shook her head in worried disbelief.

Her house of cards was in ruins at her feet.

"Found her!" Gabe's voice echoed through the empty lodge.

In the upstairs hallway Delia whirled outside their rooms toward the empty room where Patrick Mitchell usually lived. She ran down the hallway and turned left to see Gabe standing in the threshold propping open the door with his foot.

"She's inside," he said. "Dad's gotten lax about locking his door since there haven't been any guests."

Delia nodded, rage and fear a fist in her throat

that she could barely breathe around. She pushed open the door farther, and Gabe left, a soothing pat on her shoulder as he walked away.

"Josie?"

Her little girl sat on the bed, a slice of moonlight around her. Her eyes in the half-light were eerie. Glowing with hurt and indignation. The room smelled of anger, of explosive emotions, and Delia knew with one wrong move their relationship—such as it was—would blow into a million pieces that she'd never be able to get back together.

What did the divorce books say about this?

"I called Dad," Josie said, a gauntlet thrown down between them.

Delia's head spun. They'd have to go. Now. She wanted to grab Josie by the arm and drag her from this place. Run and run and run.

"What did you say?" she whispered in a voice that barely sounded like her own.

"That I'm building a fort and it's snowing and I miss him and you got a job."

She tasted blood from where she bit her lip. "Did you tell him where we are?"

Josie shook her head. "Gabe came in and I hung up."

"You shouldn't be in here, Jos."

"I wouldn't have to be in here if you'd let me use the phone."

"I told you. Dad's in—"

"Dad said that was bullshit. That you're a liar and a—"

"Watch your mouth!"

"Liar! Liar, liar, liar!" Josie leaped off the bed and threw herself against Delia, pushing at her and slapping her legs. "I hate you! I hate you!" she screamed.

"Stop it, Josie. Stop it." Delia tried to grab her daughter's hands. But Josie was quick and a year of anger gave her superstrength and Delia's legs stung from her daughter's fists.

"I want to go home. I want my Daddy."

"Jos, your father is in—"

"Why do you keep lying to me? Dad said he's not in any trouble. That he wasn't at a convention. He's waiting for me, Mom. He misses me."

"I'm sure he does. But we still can't go home—"

Josie shoved again and Delia toppled against the closed door. "Why? Why are you saying that?"

Frustration and fear bubbled over and spilled across the room. "Because your father is a bad man, Josie!" Delia cried. "He's hurt a lot of people."

"Who?"

"Well, those families in the van who died in the desert."

Again Josie's head shook. "They caught the guy that did that."

"I know." Delia dropped down to her knees, hoping to look into Josie's shadowed face. There were no books written about this situation. Her daughter wasn't found in a textbook and they were going to have to do this on their own. "But that guy was working with your dad."

"So, why didn't they arrest Dad? Huh? If he had something to do with it?"

Delia looked at the ceiling. How did she explain this to her little girl? The evil web of golf buddies, the twisted society of comrades who protected one another, the betrayal and pain that they created at others' expense. At hers.

She blinked back sudden tears. Her ex-husband. The man she'd loved and vowed to care for in good times and bad, had wrapped his fingers around her neck and tried to kill her.

"He hurt me, Josie," she finally said, sending the words she had never wanted to say into the world.

"How?" Josie asked after a moment.

Delia decided to skip the past two years of belittling, the verbal slaps and emotional punches he'd landed. Instead, she slid down on her bottom, sideways, into the white moonlight, boxed by the window.

Lifting her chin, she pulled down the high collar

of her gray turtleneck and revealed to her daughter the bruises on her neck.

She shut her eyes and prayed she was doing the right thing.

Josie's little fingers pressed the purple-black heart of the worst of the bruises and Delia winced. "What happened?" Josie asked, her voice trembling and scared, as though she was caught on some scary edge of something.

Knowing how that felt, having lived the past few weeks on that edge herself, Delia wanted so badly to pull her daughter away from that edge, away from the fall that would change everything.

But she couldn't. She had to push her over and it broke her heart more than anything Jared had ever done to her.

"He was very mad at me, Josie. Because I told him that I was going to tell the police about the man—Dave—who had been living with you."

"Why would that make him mad?"

"Because it was supposed to be a secret. You weren't supposed to know. You got up late that night you saw him, remember? You went to the bathroom and saw him on the couch."

Josie nodded.

"Well, if people knew about that, your dad would get in trouble. Big trouble."

"He'd go to jail," Josie said. It wasn't a

question, it was a statement. She got it. She understood.

"Right. And—"

"And he doesn't want to, so he did that to you so you wouldn't tell anyone."

Delia hiccuped a cry of relief. Of weary gratitude.

Josie traced the yellow edge of one of the bruises. "He's probably really sorry, Mom. He didn't mean it. He was just scared. You know how you get mad at me when you think I've run off? That's—"

Delia's relief and gratitude crashed and burned.

"It doesn't make it okay, Josie. We've told you that, haven't we? We've said there is no reason ever for another person to hurt someone who is smaller or weaker than them."

Josie nodded and Delia waited for the cosmos to give her an answer. A way to turn.

Josie's eyes were full of tears. "I'm scared, Mommy," she whispered, and Delia pulled her daughter into her arms. Hugging her tight. Ignoring the fact that Josie didn't hug her back.

"Me, too, sweetie. Me, too."

Just like that she knew what she had to do.

JOSIE HAD PASSED from fitful sleep into a deep slumber, her mouth open and slightly snoring. Her closed eyelids appeared to be bruised and it strengthened Delia's resolve.

She pulled the heavy warm blankets up higher around Josie's shoulders and smoothed back the red-blond hair that slid over her face before easing out the door of their room.

Jared might, at this moment, be on his way here, having traced Josie's call, or gathered what he needed to know from what Josie had told him, not knowing she was leading a murderer to their doorstep.

The stairs didn't creak under her feet and the chair, as she slid it away from the small bar in the corner of the dining room, didn't scrape against the floor. It was silent. Dark. She was alone. Again.

Since her cell phone was broken, she used the house phone on the edge of the bar and called her cousin, Samantha.

"Serenity House and if this is you, Jared, I've already called the cops and the next time—"

Delia closed her eyes, her worst fears confirmed. "It's me, Samantha. Delia."

"Oh my good Lord, sweetheart, what the hell is going on? Jared has had me on speed dial all night. You'd think I knew something—"

"Josie called him," she said, feeling a calm seep into her blood. This was inevitable and it felt good to not swim upstream against this decision anymore. She was giving it to God. Jared. Josie. The van of dead immigrants. Her own life. It was all in God's hands now.

"She didn't tell him where we were, other than that it was snowy. But I'm sure it lit a fire under him."

"I'll say." Samantha paused and Delia could practically see her in the cluttered office of her shelter. "You finally coming to your senses?"

"I'm not going to tell you where we are, Samantha. And I'm not going back there. He'll—" She took a ragged breath. "It's too dangerous. But I want the name and number of the private investigator you use. I'm ready to put Jared away."

"Atta, girl, Dee, I've got it right here."

"I don't know how this works. I don't have any money, right now. I mean, does he take credit cards? Does he have some kind of installment plan?"

"It's okay, sweetheart. He owes me some favors and when you talk to him just tell him you're my cousin. J.D. is the best and Jared made lots of mistakes. It will be a cakewalk for my guy."

"When did you get so dangerous?" Delia asked, her head spinning.

"When did you?" Samantha asked.

The memory of Max's lips on her throat blazed through her body. Some of this dangerous courage she owed to him. Hard to believe, impossible to put into words, but he'd proved to her that if she wanted any kind of future for Josie—for herself—she needed to do this.

Bad men did not lurk around every corner. There were still people in this world she could trust.

"I know you're scared," Samantha said. "But you're doing the right thing."

"I know." Delia nodded in the dark. At this moment, it was the only thing she was sure of.

MAX ENTERED the inn through the kitchen, unsure of whether he was relieved or worried that the network had come up with nothing regarding a possible kidnapping, or possible attempted murder in Texas involving a woman matching Delia's description.

The absence only proved Delia had never filed charges against her husband. And that her husband was not reporting Josie—if Josie was her real name—missing.

So, nothing confirmed but nothing put to bed, either.

What he needed was a straight answer from Delia. Since that was about as likely as Max taking the job Joe had brought up again tonight, he'd have to make do with whatever leftover dessert was in the fridge and a cold beer to get him through the night.

There were certain advantages to this job, he acknowledged while opening the fridge to find some kind of chocolate-caramel brownie situation, that being a cop just didn't have.

Late nights at the station were cold coffee and stale doughnuts. This was a definite upgrade.

He hit the swinging door to the dark dining room, his mind on grabbing a beer from the fridge at the bar. He didn't get two steps before he stopped.

She was here.

IT WAS HIM.

The dark shadow in the kitchen doorway was Max. Her whole body knew it.

He kissed me. That man, right there. He touched me like I was gold and he kissed my skin and he wanted me. Needed me in a way that I haven't been wanted or needed in a hundred years. If ever.

Delia held her breath, waiting in the shadows to see whether he'd notice her. Her better sense knew he needed to walk past her on his way to his cabin or out to his clearing or wherever he spent his nights.

It's what she knew. It wasn't what she wanted.

And when he walked right up to her in the dark, like a magnet, like the moon rising in the twilight sky—inevitable and solid and compelling—her foolish heart skipped a beat.

"Delia."

His low voice washed over her like warm water. He set a plate on the bar beside her and his scent curled around her—smoke and chocolate. A dangerous combination.

"Max."

"You make a habit of sitting in the dark?"

She smiled, glad the dark was so complete, the cloud cover over the moon impenetrable. She didn't want him to see her, to see what was too close to the surface, what she couldn't keep submerged after this day. "So it would seem."

"Everything okay?"

"Sure."

He paused and she could feel him in the darkness. She wondered what he was doing.

"Do you ever tell the truth?" he asked.

"Do you?"

His laugh was a low rumble that faded to a deep and thick silence. But not uncomfortable. On the contrary, it was nearly too comfortable. She should be worried. Instead, she gloried in the fact she wasn't. The only place in her life these days where she wasn't afraid, was next to this man.

After her phone call to J.D., she was still trying to get her head around the idea of surveillance and cell-phone records and paper trails.

"If Josie saw those two together, lots of people did. Your husband was cocky and cocky criminals

make stupid mistakes. And just because your friend, Chris, betrayed you doesn't mean there aren't good men in that office. We'll work this out," J.D. had said and relief had poured through her body like champagne.

Maybe she was drunk on all that relief, on the satisfaction of finally gathering her courage and doing what she should have done days ago. Regardless, she was going to let herself enjoy the way Max made her feel.

Secure.

And, she thought, remembering his lips on the flesh of her neck, his breath in her ear, the terrible need she sensed in his touch and voice, he made her feel desired beyond all reason. Deliciously so.

On the edge of what might be the end of her life, she wanted that feeling back. In spades.

Tomorrow would have to take care of itself.

She was wired with giddy nerves, unsure if what she'd set in motion would ultimately free her or kill her.

Laughter, nervous and inappropriate, gushed from her throat, uncontrollable. Her ex-husband, the man she had slept beside for ten years, the man she had made coffee for and bought fancy underwear for, the man who used to wrap his arms around her waist at concerts and laugh at her bad jokes, might try to kill her. Again.

"Delia?"

The scrape of the stool, the movement of air, indicated Max was sitting down next to her. "What happened?" he asked. "What's going on?"

"Oh Lord, Max." She laughed again. "We don't have that much time."

"I got all night."

She knew she should leave, tell him thanks but Josie was waiting for her. Which was true. But loneliness was also in that bed and she wasn't yet ready to crawl between the covers with that.

"I told Josie," she said. Staring at where she thought her hands were in the dark, spread palm down on the bar. "I showed her the bruises."

"And?"

"And…" she took a deep breath. "I just ruined my daughter's life, Max. I—" She rubbed her forehead. "I've fed her to the wolves and now she's scared and freaked-out."

"You didn't do that," he said. "Your husband did when he put his hands on you in violence."

She knew he was right, but it didn't make anything easier.

"My parents got divorced when I was a kid," she said. "My mom left, went back to France and I used to go back and forth. School years with my dad and summers in France."

"That's not so bad," he said. The smell of

chocolate was intense and the sound of his teeth against his fork sent long shivers down her spine.

"It was hell," she told him. "I was like a battleground, and they continued to fight out their differences on me. I would go to France and hear how my father was a domineering ape and I would live with my dad and hear about my mother the faithless drunk whore."

"That's awful, Delia," he said, his voice deep and low and filled with sympathy. "No kid should have to go through that. But that's not what you've done to your daughter."

"It isn't?" she asked. "Because it sure feels that way. I spent my whole life never feeling secure, never knowing what terrible thing my parents would say or do next in order to prove to me how bad the other one was. I didn't know what was true or what was false. And tonight the last thing my daughter said was she was scared. And I did that. I ripped away her security." She felt the bite of tears and couldn't breathe.

"Here," he said, and something gooey and wet hit the side of her mouth. She licked her lips and tasted chocolate. "Eat this," he ordered. "Don't cry."

She laughed and he stuck the fork and brownie right in her mouth. She had no choice but to chew and swallow. Chew and swallow one of the most delicious things she'd ever eaten.

"Wow," she muttered around the mouthful of decadence. "That's really something."

"That'll take your mind off your worries."

She chewed and considered the dark shape of the man next to her. "What is it about you, Max?" she asked. "You come around and I blab all my problems to you."

"It's the stranger-on-the-bus syndrome—you want to tell someone and I'm here."

"You're selling yourself short, Max. I think you're one of the good guys. My daughter certainly thinks so."

He was silent. The silence grew denser and deeper and she almost felt dizzy from it and the dark that wrapped around the tugging of her attraction to him. "Maybe I should be asking you why you're sitting in the dark," she said, to break the terrible quiet.

Another bite of brownie hit the side of her face and she laughed. "Distraction won't work, Max. I'm very single-minded."

"I noticed." He bumped her again with the brownie and she reached out to grab his hand and direct it toward her lips.

She felt every callus, every rough hair on his fingers. She felt the heat of him, the size. It was the most powerfully intimate thing she'd ever experienced.

The taste of chocolate burst across her lips and she licked the fork as he slowly pulled it out of her mouth.

"My mom left us when I was a kid," Max said. "Up and left in the middle of the night. Three days later Dad told us she was gone for good and that was the last time we talked about her."

"What?" She gaped at him. "You never talked about her?"

"Not until a few months ago." She heard the click and slide of the fork on the plate. "And I don't think I felt any safer than you did as a kid. I kept waiting for my dad to disappear or my brother."

"But they didn't," she whispered.

"Nope," he said. "But I was still scared, so I grew up and tried to make them leave just so I could get over the anticipation." He chuckled. "I fought and fought with them. I made it real hard for them to love me, but they never left. Even after I was—" He stopped suddenly, the heated intimacy of the room changing slightly. "What do they put in these things?" he joked, and she heard him take another bite of the brownie, forestalling what he'd been about to tell her.

She didn't push him.

She understood him so well. The night. The shared brownie. It was trouble, but she didn't want to walk away. She wanted more of it. She wanted the dark to soak her up, make her disappear for a while. Long enough to forget. Long enough to make going to bed and waking up another day doable.

"Have you ever wanted to walk away from your life? Just forget—for a little while—who you are and what you've done?"

"Sure."

She heard the click of the fork against his teeth and her stomach whirled in sudden painful desire.

"You want a drink?" he asked.

"That's not a good idea." She shook her head. The oblivion of getting blind drunk was too much work.

"More chocolate?"

"Always a good choice."

The smell of chocolate and caramel was a delicious tease and the moist cake brushed her lips, but now nothing was funny.

"Open your mouth," he murmured.

The memory of his mouth on her throat ran on a constant loop and she couldn't chase away the desire—stupid as it might be—that his lips and his touch created in her. And so she stopped trying to chase it away.

The desire fizzed through her, dilating her whole body.

She opened her mouth and he slid in a bite of brownie. She shut her eyes and sighed with pleasure, licking everything off the fork.

Sitting on the edge of her seat, she leaned toward him and his heat and the chocolate, and when she felt him move toward her again she held out her hand and caught his.

"Why did you kiss me today?" she asked.

He put down the fork and twisted his palm so it cupped hers. The contact made her breathless. She felt him shrug.

"Let's be honest," she said, forestalling whatever excuse he was going to give her. "Tonight. Please. Let's just tell the truth. Why did you kiss me?"

"Because I wanted to. I've wanted to kiss you since I saw you."

"The first time I saw you I yelled at you."

"I know, I like that in a woman. And—" He paused as if judging how much to say. "You seemed like maybe you needed that kiss. Like it had been a while since someone had tried to make you feel better."

"It has. It's been—" She shook her head "—years."

"Why'd you let me kiss you?"

"Because I'm stupidly and wildly attracted to you."

His laugh made her smile. "That's honest," he said.

"What about you?" she asked. "Has it been a while since someone tried to make you feel better?"

He pulled slightly on his hand, but she didn't let go. She slid off her stool and stood in the *V* of his open legs. "Has it?"

"I can't even remember the last time," he said. "But that's—"

She pressed her lips to the back of his hand and his fingers crushed hers for a split second.

"Delia." He sighed. Her name and nothing more. No recriminations. No *we better stop*. Nothing. Her name and a longing so powerful she knew he felt it, too.

"I just want—" She felt unsure now of the wisdom of this idea. Freedom. Forgiveness. Absolution. Forgetfulness. Mindlessness. She wanted all of that and his body against hers.

Words failed her and so she took his hand and pressed it to her face, tilted her head so her lips tasted the salt of his flesh.

"I know what you want," he muttered, and slid his hands under her arms, lifting her onto the bar. He pushed the cake out of the way, the fork falling to the floor.

His breath teased her lips and his hands stroked her sides and her whole body lit up like a Christmas tree.

"Max—"

He kissed her instead of answering her. He kissed her like she was water, cold and crisp, and he was dying of thirst. He touched her like he couldn't pull her close enough. His tongue licked hers and she gasped with the pleasure and pain of wanting someone so badly, so quickly. Blood charged through her body to parts forgotten and neglected.

His fingers stroked the skin above the waistband of her jeans and she could feel the calluses on his thumb. Nothing had ever been so erotic.

She opened her mouth. Her body. Her entire being. Her arms held him tight, her hands made fists in the long hair at the back of his collar. She pushed the jacket off his shoulders so she could get that much closer to his skin. Even that wasn't enough. Nothing was enough.

She pulled at his shirt, starved and angry that anything was in her way. Buttons flew off, pinged and rolled to stop in the darkness.

He groaned and laughed against her mouth and then nipped her lips, sucked on her tongue. He palmed her breasts—not at all gentle and she loved it. Reveled in it, returned the touch with the rake of her short fingernails across his back. She dipped her hands into the waistband of his pants, felt the muscles of his butt under her fingertips and suddenly couldn't wait to get this man naked.

Madness.

He pulled her right to the edge of the bar until she had to cling to him for balance. His palms rode the muscles of her legs until his thumbs met at her hips.

"You okay?" he asked.

"I'm dying, Max," she nearly cried, hungering for those thumbs to meet at the center of her body where it seemed all of her blood and all of her being waited for him.

"Can't have that," he murmured, and slid his hands to the fly of her old blue jeans. He pulled free the button and touched the skin of her stomach, which jumped and quivered under his fingers. The rasp of the zipper made her bite her lip against a moan.

It was so sexy. So dirty and wrong and she loved it. Felt safe and wanted and desired. She was bold, a sex goddess. Her back arched when his fingers slid into the waistband of her cotton underwear. She threw her hair over her shoulders and braced herself against the bar.

"You're so damn beautiful and brave," he murmured against her neck and his fingers slid deep into her body.

She cried out and he put his fingers over her lips. "Shh."

Her body screamed with the shock of it. Her toes curled in her ratty shoes. Her fingers gripped the brass rail of the bar and she wrapped her legs around his hips, pressing his fingers further into her.

"More," she sighed. "I need more."

His forehead, pressed against hers, was wet with sweat—or maybe it was hers, she couldn't tell. Didn't care. She just needed more.

She needed everything.

He swore and stepped away, pulling her jeans and underwear down and she lifted her hips so he could push them to her knees.

It was cold momentarily then he was back bringing the heat of the entire world with him. He kissed her belly, her thighs where they splayed over the edge of the bar. Then he bent and gave her the more she craved.

His mouth and fingers gave her all the more she could take. She arched and silent screams slid from her open lips as the universe broke apart into glittering glorious fragments, like stars. Like fairy dust. Like a million miracles.

"There you go," he whispered against her belly.

She looked down and saw the liquid flash of his eyes, the curve of his lips then he was gone.

The surprise of his absence was cold—shocking.

"What?" she breathed, sitting upright. "What's wrong?"

"Nothing." His voice was brittle. Hard. He grabbed his coat from the floor, the plate with the half-eaten brownie.

"Max." She reached out in the dark, missed his

arm but grazed his chest and felt the sweat that had seeped through his shirt. He was on fire. "Please. Let me—"

"I can't forget my life and what I've done, Delia. Not even for a minute."

MAX THREW the doors open and stalked outside, the cold air like a punch to the gut. It still wasn't enough. He considered shoving snow down his pants but couldn't slow down for that. The wind chilled his sweat but his body stayed hot. Tortured.

What am I? he wondered, kicking through a snowbank. *Some kind of idiot. Of course I want to forget. That's all I've ever wanted. All I've been doing for two years is trying to forget.*

And, oh Lord, if he'd just opened his pants and finished what she'd started, he'd be past forgetting right now. He knew it. He wouldn't even be sure of his name.

So, why not?

He broke into the clearing and dropped his coat, the plate and the brownie in the snow. He looked up at the dark sky. Not a star. Barely any moonlight. Nothing but black.

Why not have sex with her? She wanted it. He wanted it. And it wasn't that he was out of practice with taking what he wanted.

He closed his eyes and smiled grimly. The

answer was right there under the lust and raging heat of his hard-on.

He was afraid, in the end, that he would want more.

More than sex. More than a night on a bar making each other forget their woes.

He'd want everything with Delia.

CHAPTER TEN

DELIA CHECKED her watch and glanced back at her daughter's sleeping—or supposedly sleeping—body. If she didn't stir soon Delia would have to wake her or head down for JoBeth's scheduled massage before she woke.

And Delia wanted to talk to Josie before the day started. She wanted to see what last night had wrought in her little girl. If the hostility was still there, the anger and sadness or worse, the hero worship of her father.

Something in the way Josie was posed, her absolute stillness, seemed just a bit tense and not at all like a sleeping girl.

She'd bet money Josie was faking it and that didn't bode well.

"Jos?"

Josie sighed dramatically and Delia smiled. Her execution was pretty awful, but she deserved points for trying. "Josie, I know you're awake."

There was a hitch in Josie's breathing then she slowly rolled over onto her back. Her eyes were open and blinking at the ceiling.

"Sweetheart," Delia said, sitting on the edge of her daughter's bed. She didn't touch her and made sure not to sit too close, but she wished she could. "How'd you sleep?"

"Okay," Josie said, still not looking at her.

"A lot happened last night. Do you want to talk about it?" Josie rolled her head to look at her and Delia could see the aging that had happened in her little girl's eyes. The world looked different out of those eyes this morning, Delia could tell, and she'd do anything to make that go away—but she couldn't.

"Not yet," Josie said.

Delia nodded and stood, respectful of Josie's limits.

"Mom?" Josie braced herself on her elbow. "When you left for France, were you planning on coming back?"

The floor dropped out of Delia's thoughts. "Of course, honey. I was never going to leave for good. Why?"

"Did you have a boyfriend over there?"

Suddenly Delia knew where Josie was going with this and she shook her head, stepping to the side of the bed again. She stroked her daughter's arm, despite the nonverbal cues indicating she wanted no such thing. Maybe her daughter had been calling the shots a little too often lately. "I haven't dated anyone since your dad and I broke up."

Delia searched Josie's eyes for some kind of clue to how Josie was processing this, but she couldn't tell anything.

"Did your dad tell you that?" Delia asked.

Josie nodded and Delia wished, not for the first time, that her ex was here to strangle. She already felt bad for revealing the worst of Jared's crimes, she wasn't going to compound things by arguing with Jared through Josie.

"He was wrong," she said simply. "Very wrong. I love you and I loved your daddy. When we were together there was nothing more important than that."

Josie nodded but didn't say anything further and Delia didn't know if she believed her or not, but she took the questions as a good sign that Jared had fallen from the pedestal Josie had him on.

"Mom? If Daddy is a policeman, why did he do those things to you?" Josie's eyes were liquid and confused. "Aren't policemen good guys?"

No, Delia wanted to say. *The badge only makes them powerful, it doesn't make them trustworthy. And it certainly doesn't make them good.*

"Most of the time, honey." She hedged for her

daughter's benefit. She checked her watch again and winced. "I have to go to work for a little while. You can stay here and watch TV until I get back. Then we can do something fun."

"Finish Max's shed?"

To her horror she felt herself blush at the mere mention of his name. Her whole body went hot at the memory of last night. She knew she should feel guilt, something, on account of the one-sidedness of it all, but she couldn't muster the feeling up.

She'd slept like a baby, her body buzzing with life and a core-deep glow. Guilt really was the last thing she felt.

She felt intrigued and fascinated by the man. Sad, for him and whatever demons he carried. But mostly she was attracted.

If he'd thought walking away from her would somehow shame her or convince her that he wasn't worth the trouble, his plan had backfired.

Gloriously.

"If Max wants our help, sure," she finally answered, feeling like a schoolgirl at the thought of seeing him again.

What would he do? What would she say? It was deliciously high school and she loved it.

"Are you going to date Max?" Josie asked, and Delia sputtered.

"What? Honey, what makes you say that?"

"I don't know. Just seems like maybe he likes you or something."

Delia's brain was an empty vacuum. She hadn't received the script for this conversation. She didn't even know where to begin.

"I'm just saying it would be okay," Josie said, flipping the covers off her legs and getting up to turn on the TV.

"Well," Delia said, that core-deep glow spreading out into her hands, the ends of her hair. "I'm glad you approve."

DELIA HAD BEEN hoping that JoBeth would be the kind of client who liked silence while getting massaged.

No such luck.

"It's lovely here, isn't it?" JoBeth asked. "Those boys did such good work. I still can't believe they built this place with their own hands."

Delia hummed some kind of affirmative response. She couldn't vouch for Gabe, but Max was exceedingly good with his hands.

Get your head out of the gutter, she chastised herself. But inwardly she was grinning. Which was ridiculous really, considering how he'd left last night. She had a feeling he wouldn't be so reluctant to finish what was started the next time the opportunity came up.

And it would.

She was sure of it.

JoBeth's lower back and hips were a mass of knotted tissue and, Delia would bet, deep emotional scarring. She wondered if the woman had lost a baby or something.

Delia put a few drops of lavender in the oil she cupped in her palms and applied her hands to the spine and put her thumbs in the center of the knots, working them out slowly.

"My goodness," JoBeth said, lifting her head to look at Delia. "I thought these were supposed to be relaxing."

"Sorry, I'll ease up on the pressure." She ran her fingertips across the area she'd just abused. "Do you have a lot of lower back and hip pain?"

"Yes, you can tell that?"

"Sure." Delia smiled. People underestimated the power of massage all the time. "How about your stomach?"

"Sheila says I carry my stress in my stomach."

"Well, that's translating to the rest of the muscles in your core. You're a bit wound up along those areas."

"Sheila says I walk around like I'm waiting for someone to punch me in the stomach." Something in JoBeth's voice was a bit watery, and while it wasn't uncommon to have a client cry from the emotional and physical release of a massage, Delia had barely started.

"You're on vacation," Delia said, slowly working more pressure into her hands. "You shouldn't be feeling stressed."

JoBeth didn't say anything and Delia hoped it might be a trend for the remaining forty-eight minutes.

"So, how are the boys to work for?" she asked almost immediately and Delia nearly groaned. But the client dictated the session so she and JoBeth discussed the brothers and Alice and the upcoming baby.

"Now," Delia said at the end of the massage, rubbing her thumb across the bridge of JoBeth's nose and down across her cheekbones. "Be sure to drink lots of fluids and take it easy for a while today. Tomorrow you might be sore."

"I'm sore now." JoBeth laughed and opened her eyes. Delia smiled into them and stepped away from the table. She helped the older woman sit, clutching the sheet to her naked chest, and walked toward the door to give her some privacy.

"For a restaurant manager and a former cop, the boys sure do know how to give guests their money's worth. Who would have guessed—"

Delia blinked, her stomach lurching. "Who is a cop?"

"Max." JoBeth ran her fingers through her silver hair, unaware that she was pulling Delia's world down around her. "Or he was, anyway. Until that incident with the teenager."

Delia had to brace herself against the wall to stand. "What incident?" she whispered.

"Are you okay, sweetheart? You've gone quite white."

"What incident with the teenager?" she asked again, not caring how she sounded. Only caring, only thinking she'd been duped by another cop. Nausea gurgled through her and she put her fingers to her mouth.

She'd trusted another cop. Another—

"He killed a teenager," JoBeth said.

Delia gasped.

She'd trusted another killer.

DELIA MARCHED, a woman possessed, a woman in full control of her rage and anger, through the inn. Dangerous, her cousin had said, and now she believed it.

"Have you seen Max?" she asked Chef Tim in the kitchen and he looked nervous at the sight of her. "Have you?" she barked, and he hastily shook his head no.

Memories of last night, the ones that had kept

her warm all morning long, that for hours had not embarrassed or bothered her, filled her with shame.

She'd opened her legs for a lying, murdering cop. She'd practically begged him to put his bloody hands all over her.

"Where's your brother?" she asked a startled Gabe and Alice in Gabe's office.

"Max?" Gabe asked, wide-eyed.

"Do you have another one?"

"No. But—"

"Where the hell is he?" she yelled, fraying at all corners, losing her grip on everything. Thank God he didn't know where she was from or that her husband was a cop. If he had known she had no doubts, none, that Jared would be here right now.

The pain of that imagined betrayal was stunning and she gathered that up in her stomach, mixing it with the rage and lust and shame.

"Delia?" Alice stepped beside her, carefully laid a hand on her shaking shoulder, and Delia wished she could slap that comforting hand away. "Are you okay?"

"I'm fine. I'm just looking for Max."

"Did something happen during JoBeth's massage?" Gabe asked. "What is with the woman that she keeps upsetting everyone?"

Delia turned and left the office, heading for

the back door. He was probably out in his clearing anyway.

But she came to a dead stop in the middle of the kitchen—her brain turning to mush, her blood to ice water.

Her worst fears were confirmed.

Through the window of the door she saw, out in the parking lot, a brown sedan with police lights and across the doors in bloodred letters it read County Sheriff.

"WELL, I THOUGHT I'd get a good look at them myself. Get my own description of them. You know as well as I do that there are a lot shades of red hair," Joe said, sidestepping the snow Max was shoveling out of the small parking area behind the kitchen. "Unless you're planning on coming down to the office every day. In which case, you might as well take—"

"For crying out loud, Joe," Max said, leaning against his shovel. "Give it a rest. I don't want the job."

Joe just stared at him, his old eyes saying *Oh, really?* loud and clear.

"I don't." Max shook his head and went back to shoveling, sweat running down his spine, despite the cold. The furnace at work in him was churning out enough heat to keep him sweating for days. "And you better get going before this snow gets much worse. We're supposed to get a foot by afternoon."

"Well, what about the girls? Fresh reports come across the wire every day, Max. And you haven't even told me what we're looking for. If this woman is committing a crime—"

"She's not."

Guilt was feeding coal into this fire in him. He believed he'd done the right thing yesterday, investigating Delia and Josie. But now, after last night, it felt wrong.

He trusted her and wanted to help her and going behind her back wasn't the way to get that done. If she found out, she'd kill him, destroying the chance for any future kissing in dark rooms.

Something he'd been obsessing about most of last night and this morning.

He couldn't get her out of his head. Her scent was on his hands, the feel of her was burned into his skin. He wanted to close his eyes and spend the next twenty years replaying those twenty minutes in the dark last night.

But, in terms of going behind her back to Joe and the national database, it wasn't as though she'd left him with much choice.

It wasn't the most nefarious thing in the world

to protect your family, he tried to convince himself through the guilt.

But it was nefarious to lie, go behind her back, protect his family then do what he did on the bar last night.

He needed to start over with her. From scratch. And he couldn't do that while investigating her.

Max buried his shovel deep under snow and strained to fling it over his shoulder. "I got a little overeager," he told the sheriff. "But if I find out more, or the situation changes, I'll bring you in. Don't worry about it."

Joe grumbled and shoved his wide-brimmed hat down farther on his head. "You got your head so far up your ass, boy, you don't even know what the situation is."

Joe got back in his cruiser and pulled away, kicking up gritty snow as he drove off. As Max turned back to shoveling, something flashed in the window of the kitchen door and all he saw was Delia's red hair as she ran away.

He charged through the kitchen.

"Hey," Gabe said, stepping out of his office. "Delia was looking for you."

"I know," Max muttered, hitting the door to the dining room in time to see her charge up the stairs. His brother followed him.

"Delia," Max cried. She didn't stop so he tempted fate and reached for her arm. "Stop, please—"

His fingers barely grazed the flesh of her arm and she turned and smacked him hard across the face. He stumbled back a step. She was small but mighty and his whole head rang from the blow. No doubt his cheek was red, too.

Gabe, his protective big brother, stepped toward them, fire in his eyes. Max waved him away. He deserved that smack.

"Don't you dare come near me," she snapped. She turned again, heading up to her room and who knows what kind of trouble. He knew if she got away from him now, she'd be gone for good. And he wasn't ready for that. Not yet. Not with her taste still on his tongue.

He jumped around her and stood in her way.

"Delia, what's wrong?"

He didn't touch her, but he made it real clear that her little body, fueled by whatever anger she had for him right now, wasn't a match for his size.

She glared at him. "Get out of my way."

"I got all day, Delia, and you're not getting past me. So, tell me what's going on."

"What was the sheriff doing here?" she asked.

"He's a friend."

Her laugh was coated in poison. "Oh, I'll just

bet he is." She stepped right, and he mirrored her, not letting her pass.

"You're a cop!" she yelled. Her hands were fists at her sides and her eyes spit daggers at his heart. "I should have known," she cried, putting her hands in her hair, fisting them in exasperated rage.

He wanted to ease those fists, stop her from pulling her own hair, but he couldn't touch her.

"Who else gets shot?" she asked, clearly mocking herself. "Cops, criminals and soldiers. That's it. You lied to me," she bit out.

He shook his head, feeling like a member of the bomb squad and not sure which wire would calm her down and which would make her explode. "I *was* a cop. I'm not anymore."

"Don't play word games, Max."

"It's the truth." He held out his hands. "I was a cop up until two years ago."

"Okay." Her sarcasm lashed at him. "How about you tell me the truth about that scar."

They leaned forward at the same time and her fingers actually grazed his neck, leaving a trail of fire across the tissue that was just as hot as the bullet that had caused it.

"I told you the truth yesterday," he said rubbing at his neck.

She rolled her eyes. "You're so clever, aren't you?

Dodging all my questions, while getting me to answer all of yours, pretending to be so righteous."

"What do you want to know?" he asked, beginning to lose his temper. He wasn't righteous. Or clever. He was feeling awkward, lost, unsure of what she wanted. Unsure of what he wanted.

"What happened to the teenager? The kid with the gun."

Here it was. The words he didn't say. He could keep his silence, let her go, thinking the worst while he strangled on these words. Or—

"I shot him."

The words exploded out of him, startling both of them. He didn't look away from her. He didn't let either one of them off the hook. Her eyes went wide, then narrowed in disgust and horror.

"That's not the whole story, Max," Gabe cried. "You can't keep—"

"I quit, Gabe," she said, interrupting him. "You'll have to find someone to replace me."

"Max," Gabe nearly moaned. "What did you do?"

"Apparently," Max said, his eyes still locked to Delia's, "I'm a murdering cop bastard, just like, I am finally figuring out, her ex-husband."

Delia's expression shut down. "I'm leaving right now."

This time when she tried to get past Max, he let her go.

Better this way. It was always going to be better this way, with her leaving. He'd been stupid to think otherwise.

"Delia?" Gabe said.

"Let her go," Max said.

"No." Gabe shook his head, the look in his eyes the same as when they were kids—before Max got bigger and stronger than him and some bully on the playground picked on Max. Gabe, his older brother, his savior and protector, would rush in and defend him. "She's not leaving here thinking the worst of you."

"It doesn't change anything," Max said.

Gabe's eyes were so sad, they hurt as much as the judgment in Delia's. "Of course it does," he whispered, then looked over his shoulder to focus on Delia where she'd stopped on the stairs.

"Believe what you want, Delia," Gabe said. "But Max saved a woman and a baby that day and he nearly died doing it. He left the force a—"

"Don't, Gabe—"

"A hero. Damn it. Can we just talk about this? Finally. You're a hero."

Max felt his insides turn to water, his bones to air. Delia stopped on the stairs and his whole body, as it had since he'd met her, was tuned to hers and he could feel her tension. Her urge to run. Her heavy feet.

Killed. Teenager. Wife and mother. Hero.

His ears rang and the air buzzed as if gunshots had been fired.

"Max?" Delia asked, her voice still skeptical, still touched with her anger. And rightfully so.

He didn't answer. It was hard enough to breathe. Why were all these people here, anyway? Couldn't he relive his own private nightmare alone? Without his brother and the woman he feared he was falling, stupidly, in love with, as witnesses.

"I don't understand," she said. "Why did you lie about this?"

"I could tell," he whispered. "I could tell how you felt about cops and—" he took a deep breath, determined to be honest…for once "—I didn't want you to feel that way about me."

He heard her gasp. She came down the steps and he braced himself for her touch, locked himself down tight, tautened every muscle, hid away his heart. But it wasn't enough. He felt her hand on his arm in his gut, in his scrotum and brain, through his blood.

"Please, Max. Tell me what happened."

Oh God, those eyes. She was killing him with those eyes, eviscerating him. Forcing him into the light and away from his solitude. He wanted to resist this urge to let every ghost and skeleton out of his head, but he couldn't.

Suddenly, after two years, after knowing this woman a week, he wanted to tell her. Everything.

"I thought it was a pretty awful way to become a hero, so I left the force."

Don't do it, he told himself in a last-ditch effort to keep himself removed, even as the words formed on his lips. "But I'm not like your ex-husband. You have to trust me."

"I'm all out of trust," she told him.

"You weren't last night," he said. "When you told me about your folks," he clarified at the expression on her face. He understood sex often wasn't about trust. She'd as much as said that last night. What had happened between them was about forgetting. "And when you told me about your husband—that took trust. Like it or not, you trust me."

She shook her head. "That makes it worse, Max. You're right, I did trust you, knowing I shouldn't, knowing it would probably bite me in the ass. And you lied."

Her pain radiated to him, stroked him with cold fingers. He nodded.

"Maybe, I should leave you two alone," Gabe said, stepping back toward the kitchen, just as the door to the spa opened and JoBeth entered the dining room.

She looked slightly drugged and Max wondered

if that was a testament to Delia's work. "Well, hello," she said brightly into the charged atmosphere.

"JoBeth, why don't you come with me to the kitchen?" Gabe said, taking her under his arm. "We'll make you a post-massage smoothie."

But slowly, because Max never claimed to be the smartest man in the room, two plus two finally equaled four in his head.

"How did you find out I was a cop?" he asked Delia, and JoBeth paused. Gabe turned, his brow furrowed.

"She told me," Delia said, pointing at JoBeth, who blinked wide-eyed at Max.

Gabe, Max knew, had been looking for reasons not to like this woman since she'd brought up postpartum depression in front of Alice.

"How do you know about Max's career?" Gabe asked. "It wasn't national news. It barely got regional coverage."

JoBeth seemed to be gathering herself for some storm. Her smile faded and her face was taut, her whole body vibrating. Suddenly, with instincts that came with being shot, Max wanted to leave the room. Right now. Because something big was about to happen and he already felt overloaded.

"I should have been honest with you from the start," she said. "I'm not who you think I am—"

The front door opened and a cold draft blew across the room.

"Whew," Patrick Mitchell said from behind him. "It's a nightmare out there."

JoBeth seemed to crumple. Melt. Her face folded into lines of grief and pain. "Patrick," she whispered.

"Iris?" Patrick asked, his voice ravaged. "Boys? What the hell is your mother doing here?"

CHAPTER ELEVEN

"MOTHER?" Gabe asked, his tone so cold it chilled Iris's stomach. It was as she'd feared. The men in the room regarded her with such hate that frostbite settled into her bones.

She nodded, unable to talk. Unable to take her eyes off her husband. He was thicker through the chest, grayer in the temples. He still wore the old blue work pants he'd worn every day of his life, but the look in his eye…

Her breath caught on a sob. It wasn't love, the look in his eyes, but it wasn't hate.

Hi, baby, she wanted to say as if he'd come in from work and it was thirty years ago. He'd take off his coat, pull her into his arms for what wasn't so much a hug as it was a chance to lean on each other. A few minutes of bearing each other's physical load at the end of long days.

I've missed you, she thought, unable to look away. Wishing she never had, wishing she'd never so much as blinked when she was with these men. The years and regrets, her fears and anxieties fell down on her, crushing her with their weight and suffocating presence.

She felt their hate like rocks thrown at her and she gathered herself to run. "This was a mistake, a terrible mistake," she said, shaking her head.

But then, Patrick, unsolicited and unexpected, nodded. A brief dip in his chin. A light in his wet eyes. Whether it was in agreement or approval of something, of her being here, or her missing him or understanding how she felt—didn't really matter. It was enough.

Don't leave, his eyes said. *Not again. Not yet.*

The rocks cleared momentarily and she could breathe.

"Get out," Gabe said. "Pack up and go. We don't want you here."

The look in Gabe's eyes was all hatred, and all directed at her. She wavered under the intensity and felt herself diminishing, evaporating. Burning to smoke.

"Don't speak for me, son," Patrick said, and Iris could have kissed him. "I'd like to hear what she has to say."

"She's not staying, Dad." Gabe shook his head. "We told you that months ago. We don't want to see her."

"You don't want to ask her some questions?" Patrick said.

"I'll do the best I can," she said, her voice a gruff croak. "To answer everything. To explain or—"

"Explain?" Gabe cried, his face creased with outrage and horror. "How the hell are you going to explain this? You left us. Walked out. In the middle of the night like we meant nothing to you—"

"That's not true." She fought the painful tears clawing up her throat. "I know it's hard for you to believe this now, but you were my life. My world—"

"You've got a terrible way of showing it." Gabe's laugh was sharp and brutal.

She turned to gauge the hate in Max's eyes only to find his eyes totally shuttered. There was no hate. No anger. No love. No nothing and that, perhaps, was the most chilling of all.

"Max?" she whispered, worried about her sensitive boy with his dark eyes and darker shadows.

"Trust me," Gabe said, deflecting her attention from Max as he had when they were kids. "He doesn't want you here any more than I do."

"I just want to try and explain." It sounded awful to her own ears, weak and stupid. All of her speeches, the thirty years of good solid reasons she'd compiled, vanished under her tongue and all she had were these stupid clichés and platitudes.

"We don't want to hear it," Gabe stated.

"Yes." Patrick laughed nearly incredulously. "We do."

"No. She left thirty years ago and never wrote to us, never tried to come back. I'm not about to open my arms to her and pretend she didn't totally abandon us," Gabe said.

Iris turned to Patrick to see if he would feed her to the dogs on this or take up his share of the blame.

"That's not exactly true, Gabe," Patrick said.

Patrick finally shut the door behind him, and the cold wind stopped sweeping across her body.

"It's time we all had a talk," Patrick said.

Max finally moved. He walked right past her and didn't look at her, didn't seem to notice when she reached out to him, desperate to touch one of them. To feel one of her boys in her lonely arms. But he moved too fast and she was far too scared.

"Where are you going?" Patrick asked.

"Out," Max said, and even Gabe looked surprised.

"Son—" Patrick said.

Max turned and finally looked at her—his expression utterly unreadable. "Stay. Go." He shrugged. "It doesn't matter."

Then he left, the kitchen door swinging behind him.

Delia, still on the stairs, gasped and stared wide-eyed at all of them for a minute.

"Are you going to go after him?" Delia asked Gabe, and Iris could tell by the look in her eyes, the worry in her voice, that something had happened between the fierce redhead and her son. She was glad that her little boy had a protector.

"Who is *she?*" Patrick asked, pointing to Delia. Gabe simply scrubbed at his face with his hands.

"I want you out," Gabe finally said to Iris.

She felt Patrick behind her, three feet away, just as she'd felt him in those letters he'd written her years ago and then again just a few months ago.

"I've paid up for two weeks," she said, straightening her spine. "I'm not leaving a minute before then."

Gabe's eyes narrowed and he shook his head. "You pick a real strange time to be strong," he said, cutting her to the core. "We needed a mom thirty years ago. We don't need you now."

He left, heading upstairs, stomping past Delia, who waited a mere moment then went upstairs, too.

It was only Iris and Patrick in the shadowed room and she found her strength ebbing. The emotions took too much from her, and she pulled out a chair and sat before she fell down in front of him.

"So," he said, skewering her with his hard voice and ice blue eyes. He crossed his arms over his chest and she realized whatever support she might have from him was for the benefit of the boys. The united front he'd always believed parenting should be. Still the same man, despite what she'd done to him. Married to an absentee wife for thirty years. Raising those boys on his own without the help of a mate.

The pain of tears in her throat returned.

"So," she whispered, wondering where they could possibly go from here.

"I just threatened our lawyer, trying to get your address from him," he said.

"That's where you've been?" she asked.

"He didn't budge, though," he said. "I waved my fist in his face and he didn't even give me a state. Apparently, our lawyer has more of a right to know where you've been than I do."

"I knew you'd try to find me," she said. "If you knew."

"And that would be wrong?" he cried, his temper catching in his throat. "A husband shouldn't know?"

"I didn't want you to," she said, looking at her hands, unable to tell him the whole story.

"All right, how about now? Can you tell me now? Where the hell have you been?" he asked.

The timer on her watch beeped and she turned it off without looking.

"I have to take my medication, Patrick," she said, and he threw his hands in the air.

"I'll be right back. Wait for me," she said, standing on wooden legs.

"That's all I've ever done, Iris," he said, and collapsed into a chair.

DELIA OPENED the door to her room and found Josie on her stomach at the foot of the bed watching MTV. Delia never let Josie watch that garbage and Josie, when caught watching it, usually had the good grace to switch to another channel. But now she just kept watching the gyrating half-naked bodies.

"Turn that off," Delia snapped, feeling stretched too thin by all that had happened. Josie, with no real speed, reached for the remote and flicked the channel to some sitcom.

Delia leaned against the door. Her heart beat so hard it was a wonder she wasn't bouncing off the oak panel.

What is wrong with that family? she wondered, aghast at what she'd seen. How could Max possibly walk away from what had happened in that room? From his mother? *She* could barely walk away and Iris wasn't her mother.

"Mom?" Josie asked, propping herself up on her elbows. "What's wrong?"

"What isn't?" she muttered.

"Are we leaving?" Josie asked. Delia heard dread in her daughter's voice, and she wanted to scream. She couldn't stay on top of what her daughter wanted—there was no tracking mechanism anymore. She was a mystery.

"You don't want to go?"

"Well, where would we go?"

Delia let her head fall back against the door with a thunk. "Good question."

"Mom?" Her little girl's voice was ripe with a thousand terrible things. Worry, a preadolescent ennui and a pleading that had not been there. An indication that her loyalties had shifted or were shifting, or were utterly cast adrift and she was sinking fast.

I did that, Delia told herself. *I did that to my little girl.*

"It's okay, Jos," she said, forcing herself to smile. "We're not going anywhere."

"Why are you acting so weird?"

"Max and Gabe's mom is here."

"She came back? When?"

"JoBeth is their mom."

Josie's mouth fell open. "What does that mean?"

"I don't think anyone knows yet."

"Where's Max?"

She heard the solid thunk of an ax hitting wood outside. "I think he's outside."

Josie blinked at her as if to say, *Well? Aren't you going to do something?*

Delia's heart and conscience were telling her the same thing. She wanted to shrug away that feeling, ignore it and concentrate on her own little tragedies.

But she remembered him on the stairs, lost and alone, wounded by the past, raw from the present, hurt by her.

I didn't want you to feel that way about me...

And now his mother was here.

She shook her head. How could he possibly handle all of this alone?

Josie lay back down on her bed, her attention seemingly returned back to the canned laughter on the television.

Delia bit her lip and battled down her stupid instincts to go to him. She had the worst instincts in the world, they shouldn't be listened to. After all these years of listening to her parents, of marrying Jared, of not even seeing that Max was a cop, for crying out loud, it should be clear to her now that her instincts were to be ignored. Second-guessed. Snuffed out.

But she couldn't.

She'd been right about him being one of the good guys.

The urge to find Max and talk to him, when his family was clearly going to let him go out to his shed or fort or whatever the hell it was and hide, was amazingly strong.

She felt him out there like some magnetic pull on her internal compass.

Despite his act in the dining room, Max was in pain. And his loved ones were going to let him stay out there and bleed.

Hoping sense would be knocked through her skull, she banged her head against the door one more time. It didn't work.

Finding out he was a cop had seemed, on top of their intimacies, like the worst betrayal.

She knew they weren't friends. Exactly.

Or lovers. Really.

They were something in the middle, stuck in limbo. Feeling too much for the wrong person at the wrong time. But she knew, even if he didn't, that if she left now, without saying anything, without talking to him about what had just happened, it would be the betrayal.

She doubted he'd see the situation that way, but she had to look at herself in the mirror every day and in order to do that, her heart was telling her, she had to deal with Max.

"I'll be right back," she said. Her daughter waved without turning and Delia ducked out the door.

THE MUSCLES of his shoulder screamed every time he lifted the ax. He was squeezing the handle too hard and that pressure was locking down every muscle in his arms and back.

Still, he kept working.

The blazing pain in his flesh occupied him. Distracted him. Kept him from thinking about what would happen when he stopped working and the blazing pain in his flesh became a rotting ache in his heart.

Mom.

No. Don't think.

Lift. Swing. Split.

He kicked the split log into the pile at his left and picked up another section of trunk from the birch tree he'd cleared a week ago.

A week ago when he'd been working to avoid Delia. Hell, what was happening here?

No. Don't think.

Lift. Swing. Split.

He worked until his hands blistered and the pain in his shoulder seared down his back. Still, his brain kept spinning.

He should have known. JoBeth or Iris or whatever her name was, looked like him. Same dark features. Same dark eyes. That was why she had seemed so familiar. He saw shades of her every time he used a mirror to shave.

"Max?"

He spun and his shoulder screamed in fury as the ax slid out of his useless grip onto the snow.

It was Delia, of course. Red hair, blue eyes showcasing nothing but pity in them. Of course, she would pity him, after all she'd seen today. To not only find out the truth about him being a cop, but also to witness his mother's glorious homecoming.

It was pitiful. He was pitiful.

"Go away," he said. She bunched her hands in her pockets and shifted her meager weight, as if to say *I'm not going anywhere.*

"Suit yourself," he finally said. He rubbed his wrist and forearm, shaking out the pins-and-needles sensation.

"Are you okay?"

"I'm fine. I thought you were leaving."

"I changed my mind."

His heart leaped with an ecstatic glee that he ruthlessly tamped out.

"Your life isn't dramatic enough—you now want front-row seats to this circus?"

She shook her head, the long waves of her hair falling over her shoulder and he remembered touching that hair, sliding his fingers through its texture. That was only last night, but it seemed like a million years ago.

"I'm fine," he told her, and turned away to start

stacking wood, because he wasn't fine and he didn't want to look at her and fall apart.

She came up beside him and started helping him. Grabbing wood and tossing it into one of the two wheelbarrows he'd brought to the clearing earlier that day.

He could smell the scent of the lotion she used during massages—citrus and something sweet. Something dizzying.

"You don't trust me, remember? I lied to you," he reminded her, trying to thrust her out of his clearing and his life.

She blinked those big blue eyes at him, taking his abuse the way his brother and father did.

Stupid woman.

"I'm a cop," he taunted her. "Just like your husband."

"You're nothing like my husband."

Fine time for her to realize that. It didn't change anything. She was still here and he was recklessly close to his breaking point.

"I killed a kid. Shot him down. Right through the heart. Right in front of his mother and baby sister."

She was a sphinx. Silent and unreadable.

"I'll hurt you."

She smiled and shook her head. "You won't."

He wished he could prove her wrong, but she was right. He turned away, frustrated by everything, by his inability to change or control anything that was happening. Life was a train bearing down on him. He wanted out of the way but he was paralyzed. Stuck.

"I left Josie when my mom was dying," she said. "I left her with Jared for six weeks."

He shook his head, knowing what she was trying to do. "It's hardly the same thing, Delia. She left for thirty years." He felt anger swell like a balloon and fill his chest until he couldn't breathe for all the hatred. "Thirty damn years and she couldn't call or write or anything? She just shows up pretending to be someone else, pretending to be a lesbian." He laughed, but it hurt. "Maybe she is. Maybe that's why she left."

He picked up the split logs and hurled them into the wheelbarrow. "I don't even care. It wouldn't even matter."

"That's clearly not true, Max." Delia's voice was a quiet stroke to his raging temper.

"She's not my mother. She's a stranger. She's no one."

"She's your mom. And you missed her."

He shook his head and kept working. But she couldn't take the damn hint. She stood there watching him as if she had all the patience in the world and he was some temper-tantrum-throwing child.

"When I came back from France," she finally said when he wouldn't say anything, "Jared had told Josie all these lies. That I was leaving for good and I didn't want her to come with me, that I had met some other man. She believed him."

He wiped at his face. "It's not the same thing, Delia."

"Why?"

"You came back," he said, incredulous that he had to point this out to her.

"So did your mom," she said, stunning him into a sudden silence. Then, as if the day hadn't already taken enough turns, as if his head wasn't already spinning, she stepped up to him and pressed one long, sweet kiss to his cold lips.

"You should hear what she has to say. Then you can judge her all you want," she murmured against his mouth. "But you need to hear her out."

She kissed him again and he didn't do anything. Didn't kiss her back, didn't encourage her, pretended for as long as he could that she wasn't right.

But she was.

CHAPTER TWELVE

ONE MOMENT his lips were hard under hers, un-responsive and she was ready to give up. In the next moment he'd pulled her so close she was lifted off her feet.

He held her tight and his lips were soft, kissing her back.

In a sudden flash, like a light flicking on in a pitch-black room, Delia was happy. Stupid, con-sidering their situations, the heartache that seemed to meet her and Max at every turn. But there it was. She couldn't ignore it. And she didn't want to. Not right now, with his warmth seeping into her bones.

She nearly laughed at the bad timing, that she should find this man now, when she had nothing. But laughter felt like crying and she just wanted to kiss him forever.

"Okay." He sighed. "Let's go inside so I can listen to what she has to say."

"Great attitude," she joked, and for a moment it seemed as though he might get angry. Then his lips quirked in a wry smile. A heartbreaking smile. The first she'd seen directed at her. His whole face changed, the clouds lifted, the intensity that surrounded him softened, and he was magnetic in a whole new way.

He stole her breath in so many ways.

"You've got a smart mouth, Delia. I think I liked you better when you were avoiding me."

"Oh my Lord, are you…" She looked around, pretending surprise while feeling bittersweet delight. "Are you teasing me?"

His smile grew and she had to force herself to get them walking, to not spend the rest of the day out here flirting with this man, seeing what she could do to make him smile.

"I liked you better when you were making me forget my problems," she murmured, glancing at him through her lashes, like some B-movie vixen.

His eyes flared hot with a sudden desire, the memory of their encounter on the bar unspooled between them, and he squeezed her hand.

"After today I might need some of that forgetting myself," he said.

Ah, delicious, wicked and stupid temptation. She loved it.

"Well—" she winked "—you know where to find me."

He kissed her again, hard and fast like a brand.

The taste of his gratitude and respect was sweet and she could have kissed him for days, ignoring real life for as long as possible.

He turned to head back to the lodge, leaving the wood and his anger behind. He tucked her hand in his and she hung on tight.

They entered the back door and came upon Gabe staring out the window over the sink and Alice eating from a pint of ice cream as if it might run away.

"What are you doing?" Max asked, dropping her hand to approach his brother. Delia's throat went tight at the sight of the two big men, clearly grieving for their boyhoods without a mother.

"Well," Alice said around a mouthful of ice cream. "Gabe is pretending his mother isn't in the other room and I'm stress eating."

She reached under the counter she was sitting on and opened the cutlery drawer to pull out a spoon and hand it to Delia. "Join me."

Delia didn't need to be asked twice. She understood the profound therapy to be found in pints of Ben & Jerry's. Cherry Garcia got her through her divorce. Chunky Monkey saw her through her mother dying.

She hiked herself up on the counter beside Alice and dug in.

"We've got to do this," Max said to Gabe, who,

Delia realized, was barely holding back tears while Alice was steadily crying into the ice cream. "Even if it's just to say we're done—"

"I'm already done." Gabe scowled. "I've been done for years."

"You know that's not true," Max said. "Until Dad brought her up a few months ago we never even talked about Mom. You and I got into a fight last summer because I mentioned her."

Gabe sighed and wiped the side of his face with his shoulder. "I don't want to."

Max smiled and Delia's heart lifted and hurled itself against her chest, struggling for the freedom to follow its own inclinations.

Bad idea, she warned herself. *Bad idea to care for this man more than you already do.*

But, she feared, it was too late.

"Okay," Gabe finally said. "But I don't have to be nice to her."

"Absolutely not," Max agreed.

Gabe came over and braced himself against the counter so his wife could feed him a bite of ice cream.

"I love you," he told her, and leaned down to kiss the bulge of her stomach. "You, too, baby."

"Do you want me to come?" Alice asked. She put her spoon in the container and awkwardly lifted herself to hop off the counter, but Gabe stopped her.

"I want you to sit here and eat some ice cream and put your feet up," he told her, lovingly brushing a curl off her forehead. "I want you to think nonstressful thoughts and keep growing that baby. You don't need this tension right now."

That was what marriage was supposed to be, Delia thought, watching them. A good marriage has kindness and respect and appreciation. Delia looked away so she wouldn't cry, only to meet Max's earnest eyes.

Kindness, respect and appreciation were all right there.

"Thanks," he said, and she nodded, her throat clogged with emotion. "I mean it, for getting me out of that clearing and last night—"

She pushed him away, literally braced her hands against him and steered him toward the door. The world was spinning so fast she couldn't even make sense of it. Putting last night or today into words would make her have to think about it and she simply wasn't ready.

"Go," she said.

Then they were gone.

"What did you do?" Alice asked, picking up her spoon again. "You're like a miracle worker or something."

"I don't know," Delia said, and shrugged. She took the pint when Alice handed it to her and dug for a peanut butter cup. "I just went out there and talked to him."

"What did you say?"

"That he should do this. That it was the right thing." She shrugged. "Isn't it?"

"Hell, yes. I've been saying it for years." Alice squinted and pointed her spoon in Delia's face. "I have the feeling we're going to be spending a lot of years together, Delia, trying to get these Mitchell men to do the right thing."

Delia's emotion and battling heart fell to her feet and she couldn't even come up with a platitude. A half lie that would allow her to believe, just for the rest of the day even, that what Alice said was true.

That she had years here. Even a few months.

She didn't. She might not even last the week.

"I'll be leaving," she said, her honesty pouring out unfettered. "Probably by the end of January. Maybe sooner. This was never going to last. I was always going to leave."

It felt good to say it. To admit this truth she hid from these kind people.

"Why?" Alice asked.

"My husband isn't dead. It's complicated." She stopped, not wanting to implicate this family further. "I have some loose ends I have to tie up with him and my daughter wants to be home and I think that might be best. I—"

Alice's warm smile vanished. Her eyes went cold and she laboriously pushed herself off the countertop. "Does Max know this?"

Delia shook her head.

"Then go now," Alice said. "Don't you dare hurt that man any more than he's been hurt."

IRIS'S HANDS SHOOK. Her mouth was dry. Panic clawed at her like a wild animal and she hadn't even opened the door to the lodge yet.

Do this, she told herself. *Do it or you'll hate yourself forever.*

She pulled open the door and walked into the dining room to find Patrick right where she'd left him. Alone in a sea of empty chairs. She hoped maybe his anger had faded in the minutes she'd been gone and this conversation might be civil, kind even.

"Patrick, thank you for waiting."

He stood and faced her. His beautiful blue eyes that once had looked at her with such affection and kindness, such warmth and, in the end, worry, were stormy. Now he regarded her as a stranger, a problem he had to deal with.

"I want to know where you've been, Iris," he said, anger lacing his voice. "Why you sent your letters through our lawyer, as if you didn't want me to find you."

"I wanted to come back on my terms."

"So?" he asked. "Where were you and your terms for the past thirty years?"

From the kitchen her boys arrived and she, like any mother, despite the circumstances, despite the anger that rolled off them in waves, was simply happy to see them.

My boys, she thought with the pride only a mother, even an absentee one, could have.

"I've been in Arizona." She swallowed. "I was with my sister, then I met Sheila."

"Sheila?" Patrick asked, while Gabe and Max flanked him.

"She's...I cleaned her house. Then she became my doctor and I became her nurse." She shook her head. "It's complicated."

"Are you really lovers?" Gabe asked, and Patrick's jaw dropped.

"No," she said quickly. "It was a joke. A bad joke. We're just friends."

"Why are you back now?" Max asked, crossing his arms and looking every bit the hard-nosed cop he'd been.

Iris shrugged off her coat, as if taking off her armor. She stood in from of them, this firing squad, feeling naked, as vulnerable as she'd ever felt, with what little pride she had left. "It's the first time your father would let me come back," she said and tried not to feel such glee when the boys turned astonished eyes to their father.

"What is she talking about?" Max asked.

Patrick opened his mouth to tell his version and Iris decided she was going to tell this story her way. They could believe what they wanted, but she wouldn't constantly be painted the villain.

"Three months after I left I wrote to Patrick and told him I wanted to come home. That I was…better. Your father told me to stay away."

"Dad?" Gabe asked. "Is this true?"

"Better?" Max asked, his dark brow furrowing.

"She left," Patrick said, defensive. Like a brick wall, no one could convince him he was wrong. "Was I supposed to just let her come home after she'd decided she missed us?"

"Yes!" Gabe cried.

"Were you sick?" Max asked her, his attention unwavering. "Is that why you left?"

"In a way," she hedged. Her stomach drew up into knots and it was so hard to breathe. Not even her medication could control this anxiety.

"In what way?" Max asked. "How about a little up-front honesty for once, Mom." His sarcasm and temper, quick and hot like a flare gun, stunned her. She hadn't seen this side of him since being here.

"You don't remember?" she asked.

"Remember what?" Gabe scowled. "You took us to the park. We had spaghetti for dinner, you told us a knock-knock joke and in the morning you weren't there. That's what I remember."

"You cried a lot," Max said, shaking his head, as if he couldn't do the math that was right in front of him. Right in front of all of them. "You would stand at the kitchen window and cry."

She nodded. It was the tip of the iceberg, but it was part of it. But she found the words difficult to say. To open these old wounds was harder than she thought.

She opened her mouth, but no words came out, only a struggling gasp.

"You were just kids," Patrick said, his voice softer, naked without the anger and blame. "You wouldn't have understood or remembered." His eyes were wet and it hurt her to see the pain still so fresh.

"Understood what?" Max cried.

Patrick put his trembling hands on their shoulders and they turned to him, their father. She was the outsider.

"Dad?" Gabe asked, concerned, when Patrick seemed to falter.

"You wouldn't have understood that your mother was sick. Not physically, but mentally. I worried every day that I would come home and find her—" He swallowed. "Dead. Or worse, dead, and you boys hurt. She was so sad all the time and I was so scared."

"I was depressed," she supplied, and all eyes swung to her. "Clinically depressed with suicidal tendencies."

Gabe and Max rocked on their heels. Patrick tried to shore them up, as he probably had for thirty years, but Gabe collapsed into a chair, his face ashen. They were openmouthed with shock and she could see them searching their brains for buried clues, hints that the mother they'd loved had been so damaged.

"I left because I was so worried I would hurt you. Or scare you," she tried to explain. "I couldn't live like that anymore. I went to Arizona for three months and in that time I met Sheila and she diagnosed me and put me in touch with a support group and medication that helped. And, I tried to come back. Twice."

"Twice?" Gabe cried.

"And you said no?" Max whispered to his father, shaking his head. "Did you even think about us?"

"Of course I did," Patrick said. "You're all I thought about. She wrote again a year after she left and by this time, we'd figured things out. We were doing okay." Patrick was practically pleading and while she thought she'd feel satisfaction, all she felt was more guilt, more pain, more love. "And I had time to realize how hard it had been before she left." Patrick looked at her. "It was easier with you gone. We were happy again. We'd moved on. That's why I said to stay away that second time. Because I couldn't do it again. I couldn't bring the worry and fear back into our lives."

He didn't pull his punches and she was shattered by his words, though she'd always suspected that was the case. It was why she hadn't pushed, why she had let him make that decision. Because she'd already hurt him enough.

The room echoed with silence. It pounded against her eardrums like a heartbeat.

"Why are you back now?" Gabe asked.

"Sheila got sick and I realized—" she shrugged, feeling selfish for bringing this into their lives so she could have peace of mind "—I could die. One of you could and we'd never..." She shook her head. "I'd never know you. I'd never know your wives and children, and I want to. I want to know you."

There, she thought, *I said it.* Her intentions were out there for them to shred and throw back in her face.

We don't want to know you, she thought Gabe would say. *You're too late.*

Instead, they all stared at her.

"Have you always suffered from depression?"

Max asked, his eyes narrowed as if working on a puzzle.

Her blood went cold. She wasn't ready for this. She'd made promises that she wanted desperately to keep, but she couldn't lie anymore.

"No," she answered carefully, "though I have been on antianxiety medication for the past few years."

Patrick looked at her, his eyes sharp, and she knew it was over.

I'm so sorry, Jonah, she thought. *But I have to do this. I can't lie to them anymore.*

"You'd gotten depressed with the pregnancies," Patrick said. "But that was years before you left. Max was six. You'd been so good for so long. It was just the last couple of months…"

She could see them all realizing the truth and not wanting to. Gabe closed his eyes on a whispered curse.

Max slowly approached her. "You told Alice you suffered from postpartum and term depression."

She lifted her chin and found the courage to say, "I was pregnant when I left."

Patrick staggered backward and Gabe was there to help him find a chair, urging him to take deep breaths.

"You have another son," she told her husband. "Jonah. He's thirty and he asked me not to tell you."

Patrick's thick shoulders heaved with racking sobs and she stood, desperate to be near him. But Max, her warrior son, got in her way.

"You should go back to your room," he told her, his eyes obsidian with rage. "You've done enough."

He turned then, standing side by side with his brother to protect their father—a unit. A family she had no place in.

The tears she'd controlled until now slipped down her cheeks, hot with regret, burning her.

And, as she'd done before, she left because she thought it was the right thing, because she thought they'd be better off without her.

CHAPTER THIRTEEN

THE LODGE WAS silent. Dad was in his room. Gabe and Alice were in their room. Alice had taken the news about their unknown brother hard and Gabe was trying to keep her relaxed and calm. The last time Max had seen him, Gabe looked torn, pale and scattered.

And Max couldn't stop pacing.

He strode from the bar to the front door to the big window. He gazed out at the clearing, at cabin four with its front window aglow.

Mom.

He couldn't even think the word without his lip curling, his eyes narrowing.

A creak on the stairs spun him around, Delia's name on his tongue, but it was nothing. The shadows at the top of the stairs didn't change. No fiery woman emerged, calm and knowing. The lodge just settled into its foundation.

He rubbed his forehead and tried to gather

234   A MAN WORTH KEEPING

himself, tried to find some task that needed doing, some work to empty his mind. He couldn't. He felt raw and naked.

He paced and wished Delia was here. He wanted to talk to her, feel her hand on his, listen to her say something calm and smart that would actually make him feel better. That would anchor him in this new world.

He turned to continue his circuit to the window and came face-to-face with Sheila. They stared at each other across five feet like soldiers on opposing sides.

"Are you checking out?" he asked.

She shook her head. "We're booked in for two weeks. Iris wants to stay."

"She can stay," he said, "but she's not welcome."

Sheila tilted her head and smiled sadly. "You think she doesn't know that?"

Guilt reared its unwanted head.

"What she's done to us is inexcusable," he said, trying to beat back that guilt.

"She knows that, too." Sheila sighed and tucked her hands in the back pockets of her pants. "But I want to tell you what she won't."

Max wished he could kick her out, send her on her way, but he wanted to hear this. He wanted to make sense of what Iris had done, as stupid as that was. He and his brother and father had lived with a lot of blanks over the years and now was the chance to fill them. To complete some of what he'd never thought would be completed.

"Your mother arrived in Arizona a mess," she said, and Max was arrested by the woman's tone and her sympathetic, knowing eyes. "She was terrified, depressed. She had uncontrollable impulses to hurt herself and the baby she was pregnant with. So, I got her on some medication that helped and—" Sheila bit her lip then smiled "—what a change. What a woman she was. Bright and funny and a fighter. She was fierce in her opinions and her decisions. But with the letters from your father, that woman started disappearing. And in her place was a shadow. A fighter who didn't fight. She had Jonah and part of her was reborn, but she was never the same."

Max swallowed and turned to look out the window. He could practically feel his mother's pain reaching out to him, through the glass and cold air.

"I'm glad she found you," he said and, oddly, felt better for saying it.

"You remind me so much of her," Sheila said. "After she got those letters from your dad, when Jonah was a baby."

"A fighter who isn't fighting?" he said.

It was him exactly.

He blinked up at the ceiling, trying to make

sense of what he felt. Things were moving in him, giant tsunamis of emotion and a longing to not be who he was right now. Stuck waiting for the universe to push him around, trying not to care, trying not to live.

"She's in our cabin doing the same thing you are," Sheila said. "And you have every reason to be angry with her. To not like her, but don't doubt for a minute that she didn't suffer those years, too."

There was nothing he could say, so he stayed quiet, wondering who he was, right now. This moment. He heard Sheila leave, felt the draft of cold air across his neck before the door shut and the room was silent again.

His mother was clearly choosing to fight for them, finally.

But what did *he* want to fight for?

He looked up the steps, to the shadows at the top and thought of Delia and Josie.

You know where to find me, she'd said, giving him every indication that these startling feelings he had for her, this connection he felt, was reciprocated.

You know where to find me.

He did. And he couldn't wait any longer.

He took the stairs two at a time, unsure that was the right thing to do, only knowing he needed to do it.

He knocked quietly on the door, aware of the time and the young girl possibly asleep in the room. He heard sounds of the television turned low. The door opened and in the crack of the door was Delia.

Her trim body was lit by the lamplight behind her. He could see the yellow trail of the bruises around her neck just over the edge of the gray turtleneck she'd worn a few times since being here.

He wondered, idly, what she usually wore when not covering bruises. The boy in him hoped it was low cut and that someday he'd get a chance to see it.

Then he noticed that her hair was piled on her head in some haphazard hairstyle and her eyes were red-rimmed, as if she'd been crying.

"Delia?" he asked, bracing one hand on the door. "Are you okay?"

"I'm fine," she said, her sparkle, her glow and light gone. "How are you? Everything okay with your mom?"

Something was not right.

"Fine," he said, his mind already forgetting that problem and pulling toward whatever had upset Delia. "Why are you crying?"

She bit her lip. "Josie's asleep, Max. I need to go."

Delia tried to shut the door but he stopped it, his hand splayed flat. "What's changed?" he murmured, confused and suddenly worried, deep in his gut. Finally, her eyes met his and the pain there mirrored his own. For a moment there was no one in the world but them. No mother, no unknown brother, no bereaved father. No one but her.

"Nothing's changed, Max," she whispered. "That's the problem."

Then the door shut in his face.

It's late, he told himself, trying to close the yawning hole opening up in his chest. *It's been an intense day. Tomorrow we'll be able to talk. Tomorrow everything will be okay.*

THE NEXT MORNING, exhausted and on edge, Max stared at the cold coffeepot as if it had punched him and insulted his father.

"Is it too much to ask for one cup of coffee!" he yelled to a totally empty room, hoping someone was around who had a working relationship with the coffeemaker.

"We're in here," Alice called out and he quickly found her and Gabe in the dining room, sitting on the couch in front of the cold fireplace. They both wore black. Alice's sweater stretched taut over the mound of her belly.

Everyone was so damn morose. It was a funeral in every room.

"Hey," he said, slapping his brother on the back, before sitting in the chair beside the couch.

"How are you doing?" Alice asked, looking wan.

Gabe looked the same, as if he'd spent a long night staring at the ceiling, just as Max had.

"All right," Max said. "Have you talked to Dad?"

"Briefly, last night." Gabe sighed. "He's better."

Alice reached over and stroked Gabe's face and neck, a comforting partner in these grim days. Max suddenly felt more alone than he'd ever felt.

He felt the kind of alone he had wanted to feel weeks ago.

Before Delia and Josie showed up. Before Iris.

Before he had started to smile and laugh again, before he remembered what happy felt like.

"What about Iris?" Max asked, unable to say *mother*.

"Their car is still here," Alice said. "So, she must be in her cabin."

"I'm tempted to go over there and haul her out," Gabe snarled.

"I think we should give her a chance," Max said, surprising all of them.

"What?" Gabe asked. "Are you kidding?"

"I'm not saying we should forgive her, but—" he shrugged "—I don't think she wanted to hurt us. I don't think she's a cruel person, I think she did the best she could."

Gabe and Alice blinked at him, stunned.

"That's my opinion," he said, and luckily the

phone rang and Gabe picked up the extension on the end of the bar.

"Riverview Inn," he said. "Hello?" He paused. "Hello?"

Finally he hung up. "That's the second hang-up today. But word's gotten out in town that there is a massage therapist here. Delia's whole day is booked. Even Daphne is coming."

Max wanted to ask about Delia, but he wasn't ready for their questions and sideways looks.

Why? Why her? Why now?

He didn't have any answers. He felt something for her that he had never felt before. Something past the overwhelming need he'd had to protect Nell, and the infatuations and lust he had experienced in his twenties.

Delia had lied to him, was avoiding him, had pushed and bullied him into doing things he didn't want to do and yet, he liked her.

Liked her, liked her.

Despite that shut door in his face, which he was sure she would explain when they saw each other. Maybe she felt as awkward as he did, as up in the air and vaguely embarrassed by this connection they felt.

She, after all, had to try and explain the situation to a little girl.

"Have you seen Delia?" Max finally asked,

feeling an utterly inappropriate grin crease his face. Gabe and Alice's faces both turned angry.

"She's still here. For the moment," Alice said.

"What do you mean?"

Alice reached over and grabbed his hand. "You should talk to her."

He nearly rolled his eyes. Did everything have to be so hard?

"Why don't you just talk to me," he urged.

Alice and Gabe shared a quick look and Gabe shrugged, giving Alice the go-ahead to say whatever she thought she knew and Max felt again that door in his face, the strange and unwelcome certainty that *that* was the answer to his questions about Delia.

"She told me that she wasn't planning on staying past January," Alice said. "She never told any of us the truth."

He absorbed that like a blow to the stomach. "When did she say that?"

"In the kitchen yesterday, when you guys went to talk to your father and Iris."

A wave of numbness washed over his body as he remembered her telling him she was here for a fresh start.

It hurt. Not that she'd lied—that wasn't surprising. He'd come to expect that. He didn't even know her real last name, for crying out loud. What hurt, like a thousand pinpricks to his heart, was how much he'd wanted to believe her, to give her that fresh start.

He stood, suddenly needing to be outside, to find the lonely place inside of himself that didn't ache and itch with all that he wanted. And couldn't have.

"Max," Gabe said, grabbing his hand as he walked past him, but Max shook it off, the touch feeling like barbed wire.

"I'm so sorry," Gabe said. "We liked her, too."

"Come get me when Dad comes out of his room," Max said, and headed out the door to the peace of his clearing.

What a fool, he told himself, breathing deep of the cold air, hoping to get enough in his lungs that his chest might freeze up and he'd feel nothing.

Both of them were fools.

He remembered her eyes two nights ago, her whispered sighs on the bar, the touch of her lips against his in the clearing as she convinced him to confront his past.

She felt something for him, too.

She just wasn't going to fight for it.

Story of my life, he thought bitterly.

Sadly, the peace of his clearing was compromised.

An eight-year-old girl, painfully like her

mother, wearing a pink coat, sat cross-legged in the skeleton frame of his shed.

He allowed himself to hang his head for just a moment, before he faced her head-on, because that was the only thing to do with these women.

"Hi," he said, bracing himself against the frame.

She waved. Back to being silent.

"You here to work?" he asked.

"Sure."

"Well, let's get to it."

He turned toward the locked box he kept his tools in at night. Hopefully he could keep her busy and quiet.

"That old woman's your mom, huh?" she asked.

"Yep." Just the word *mom* raked him, burned and scratched at his fragile skin. To think she'd been out there, making dinner and kissing scratches and helping this Jonah with his homework while he and Gabe had been trying to make do without her.

"Are you mad?"

"Yep."

"I'm mad at my mom, too."

"Why?" he asked, and winced. Talk about unlocking doors he didn't want to open.

"Lots of reasons," she said. "She's a liar and she's mean—"

"Your mom?"

"You don't know her that well." She sneered. "She left me, too, you know. Went to France and she was never going to come back. And my dad said she—"

"You don't believe that," he said, not totally surprised to see this animosity and anger. She'd been through so much, that her not being angry would be worrisome. "Your mom loves you."

"Then why did she drag me here?"

"I think she wants you to be safe."

"I was safe at home."

He wondered if Delia knew this poison was at work in her little girl. If she didn't nip it in the bud, there'd be bigger problems down the road.

But not mine, he reminded himself. *Not my problem at all.*

"Well, maybe you'll be going home soon," he said. *Probably sooner than you think,* he thought.

The little girl fell uncharacteristically quiet and Max turned around to see if she was still there. She was and she looked at him through older eyes. Eyes that sent chills through him.

"You like her, don't you?" she said. "You like my mom."

"Yep," he answered, his ability to lie shattered.

"That sucks."

"Yep."

He tried to lock her out, shove away his unruly

feelings, but he felt Josie's little hand on his hip and her arm came around his stomach.

She hugged him.

Lost. Alone. Scared.

And she held on to him.

His throat and eyes burned, his heart ached, and his chest was too tight, too full.

This is not mine, he wanted to cry. *I can't have this.* He put his arms on her shoulders to shift her away. As if she could sense that was his intention she held on tighter.

Then he dropped to his knees and hugged her, too.

IRIS OPENED the door to her cabin to find Patrick on her doorstep, his hair silver in the bright winter sunlight, his cheeks red from the cold. Despite the years and the injustices and the animosity that sparked to life between them, she felt that old jump in her heartbeat.

Her hormones let her know she wasn't dead yet. She was foolish, but she was still a woman who'd been faithful to a ghost and a memory for a very long time, no matter how crazy that seemed.

He was a good-looking man who'd aged well. She imagined Matt Damon would look like Patrick when he was older. Gabe certainly would.

"Iris," he said. That was it. His squinted eyes were flinty.

"Would you like to come in, Patrick?" she asked, standing sideways to let him pass. Sheila was getting a massage so they would have the one-room cabin to themselves, but he shook his head.

"You want to walk?" he asked. "It's not as cold and—"

And it's easier not being in the same room as you. He didn't say it, but he didn't have to. She felt the same way. As if no matter what the square footage, no matter how high the ceiling or how many windows, the room felt crowded with all their baggage.

"Let me grab my coat," she said, pulling the brown quilted monstrosity off one of the armchairs.

"You still have that thing?" he asked.

"My pet?" she asked, using his old name for the ugly coat.

His smile was wan, reluctant, indicating there were going to be no sweet talks about the old days. Good enough, she thought, shrugging into the coat and shutting the door behind her. She barely recognized the woman in the good old days.

"There's no real need for a winter coat where I am in Arizona," she said as she let Patrick lead the way along the shoveled path toward the gazebo and the view of the Hudson River.

He shoved his hands in his pockets, curving his shoulders like the football player he'd been.

"We need to get a divorce," he said, and her head snapped around, the useless romantic memories of their youth draining away. "Put an end to this farce."

"It was your choice not to have a divorce," she said, feeling oddly panicked, as though without that marriage her life would be somehow different, which was ludicrous, but the panic was there all the same.

"I know." He shook his head. "I just always believed I was married to you, no matter where you were."

"And that's changed?" she asked.

He blinked rapidly and finally turned to her as they crested the hill. "You kept my child from me, Iris. I understand that your depression made you do a lot of things you wouldn't have done otherwise. I recognize that but I can never forgive it. Ever. I hope that you've found relief from those demons."

Tears burned her eyes. She'd never expected understanding. Not really. Not after what she'd done. Perhaps with time, understanding could turn to forgiveness. If he was willing to make the first—

"But, it's been thirty years and you kept my son from me," he said, the leash he'd always kept on his emotions slipping. "The boys have a brother they don't know. A mother who would do that… Frankly, I don't know you. I don't know the you that could do that to me."

She nodded, the tears vanishing.

"So, you want a divorce," she said.

"I mean, it's about time, isn't it?" He laughed bitterly at both of them. "I've been faithful to you for thirty years, Iris."

"You have?" she asked, shocked. "I thought you would have met someone," she said, then stuttered, the thought utterly abhorrent. "A companion." She was at a loss for the right word. "A friend or…something."

"When?" he asked. "In the beginning when the boys were little, I didn't have time or the inclination to bring another woman into our lives." He shook his head as if he couldn't believe the years he'd wasted. "There was one woman, but I ended it. She was looking to be married, to have a family and I would never have been able to give that to her. Or to any other woman."

"I was faithful, too, Patrick." Like looking into a crystal ball, she could see the last time they had touched in his eyes as if the memory was up-front in his mind as it had been in hers, played and replayed during every lonely night for the past thirty years. Unembellished and unchanged despite the years, because that night, that summer night in the backyard, with the boys asleep in their room, while they sat under the light of the half-moon, had been perfect.

Her heart surged and she wanted to reach out to him, to touch the only other person who shared that wonderful memory with her. She missed him, missed his touch, his kiss. Because, for her, forever, their lovemaking had been beautiful.

They'd conceived Jonah that night.

It was on the tip of her tongue to tell him that, but he'd suffered enough, and those details would be salt in the wounds.

Patrick blinked and the memory vanished. In its place was an angry man, wounded and pushed too far.

"I'm Catholic," he said, "but I believe my God will understand that I can't stay in a marriage with you. Not anymore."

"Okay," she whispered, nodding, feeling her bones might break under the grief they both carried.

"But why didn't you just sign the papers years ago, when I filed the first time?"

"I don't know." He shrugged, a man unsure of anything. "Because my faith forbids it. Because my conscience forbids it. Because I thought someday you would come back. I don't know."

She wanted to tell him that she *was* back. But she was years too late. "I can refile and send the papers to you."

Patrick turned and kept walking up the hill toward the gazebo. She slipped slightly on the snow and ice and he grabbed her, steadying her, then dropped his hand as if she were on fire.

But she could feel him, there on her skin, under the coat that he'd always hated. Just like she'd always felt him.

They stepped onto the cement floor of the gazebo, where the wind had cleared the snow, creating drifts against the railing.

"I used to come up here and read those letters you sent me," he said, staring at the green-gray river with its snowy banks. "Why didn't you tell me about Jonah in the letters?"

"He asked me not to."

"Does he even know about me? About his brothers?"

"When he was five he started asking where his father was, so I told him. And you have to understand, Jonah and I…" She paused, unsure how to put this into words. "We're very close, and even as an infant he knew his own mind. He'd make a decision and that was it. There was no negotiating or cajoling. What he decided was the way it was. When I told him about you he asked me if I wanted his daddy back. I said no."

Patrick sucked in a breath and she pressed on. "I said no because I didn't want him to think I wasn't totally happy with our life. I was working, he was going to a nice school, we had a little home. And, like you and the boys, we were making it work. So, when I said no, he said no. He didn't want to meet you. He was five going on thirty-five and I didn't want him to be upset."

"Very noble," he said, sarcastic.

"I know I've made mistakes," she snapped. "I get it. But you aren't without blame, Patrick. You told me not to come back twice. What was I supposed to do? Keep begging?"

"You could have told me the truth! I would have wanted my son!"

"But not me," she cried. "Not the damaged woman you married."

He paused, looked away, and that was more answer than she could bear.

"I would have taken you back," he said stiffly, telling her everything she needed to know about how that would have gone.

"You think I could live like that?" she asked. "Blamed and unloved every day? By the man I loved?"

"You have a terrible way of showing it."

"So do you."

They stood there, a million miles, a sea of stormy treacherous waters between them.

"I want to meet him," he said.

She shook her head. "I can't force him to do that."

"I want to talk to him."

"He's very stubborn, Patrick. And I think—"

"I don't care what you think. He's my son and I have to talk to him. If I have to chase him down in Arizona, I'll do it. My boys will do it."

It was true, she'd always known it was true. It was why she'd hoped, foolishly, that she would never have to tell Patrick about Jonah.

"Okay," she conceded. Jonah would do it for her. Her baby would do just about anything for her, which is why she made sure she never asked for anything. He'd ruin himself to make her happy.

"What's he like?" Patrick asked.

She smiled affectionately. There were few words to describe Jonah.

"He's driven and stubborn, like I said. Intensely loyal, and that can make him unforgiving. But he's brilliant, principled and compassionate in his own way."

"Is he happy?" Patrick asked, frowning, and Iris realized her description of Jonah was rather stern. And he was rather stern.

Iris nodded. "Sometimes. Growing up without a father was hard for him, Patrick. He was always small. He was sick often. I think he's always thought of himself as a bit of an outsider."

"What does he do?"

Again, Iris wasn't sure how to say this. "He's in investing. Banking sort of things. And building."

"Building, like me?" he asked. And while what Jonah did was nothing like what Patrick did, she nodded.

Patrick stared out at the water, clearly grieving, clearly wishing he could have been there to ease the burden her little boy had carried at such a young age.

"He has your smile," she said. "And now, as an adult, he reminds me of you and Gabe in social situations. He can be very smooth and charming."

He smiled, bittersweet and slightly forlorn, and she found herself caving in, hoping the decision would be good for all of them.

"I'll call him and he'll come," she said, and Patrick's eyes closed in relief.

"But only if I'm here. He won't come otherwise."

Patrick went very still and she felt herself mirror that stillness, waiting for his anger or understanding.

"Okay," he said, turning to her, his cheeks red, his eyes dry. "Stay. Just get my son to me."

CHAPTER FOURTEEN

MAX KNEW when to admit he was in over his head. Daphne had brought her six-year-old Helen while Daphne went in to get a much-needed massage from Delia. He, because he was stupid and trying to avoid Delia and keep Josie occupied, had taken Josie and Helen to the clearing to facilitate some little-girl bonding over the diligent application of sandpaper to wood.

In his defense, he'd thought the activity and the company would help Josie, who had been getting moodier and moodier. But he hadn't realized how badly things were going until Josie knocked Helen down in the snow.

Josie had immediately apologized, crying far harder than Helen did, who had been simply startled. But he marched both girls back to the inn.

"I'm so sorry," Josie said again. Her little hands were fists at her sides and Max had the distinct impression that she wanted to hit herself most of all.

Bad forces were at work in that little girl.

"It's okay," Helen said, holding tight to her mother's side. Daphne patted Helen and, because Daphne was just that kind of lady, she reached out to hug Josie. "Why don't you come up to the farm someday?" she said, and gave Max a smile over Josie's head. "We'll do something more fun than construction."

Max wanted to say that Josie wouldn't be here long enough to have any playdates but it didn't seem like a good time.

Daphne and Helen left, going through the kitchen to talk to Tim about their produce order since Daphne was their organic fruit and vegetable supplier.

"Well," he said, turning to Josie.

"Don't tell my mom," she said quickly, her eyes pleading, which was the first normal kid reaction he'd seen from her since Delia had revealed the truth about Josie's dad.

He chewed his lip. It was obvious the kid felt bad and wouldn't do it again. Should Delia find out, she'd freak out and that wouldn't do any good. "Tell you what. I have to talk to your mom, but I won't tell her exactly what you did."

Her face lit up. "Thank you, Max—"

"But you're going to have to," he said. "Sooner or later."

The lights in her eyes dimmed slightly, but she was still grateful. "Thanks," she said. "I really am sorry."

"Do you know why you did it?" he asked, and she stood there, so still. So careful, as if any movement might lead her down a path she didn't want to go. "All right," he said, ruffling her hair. He checked his watch. "Why don't you go on upstairs and watch some TV. Your mom will be up in a second."

She nodded and was gone in a flash. Max turned slightly toward the spa door.

He was happy to have a reason to seek Delia out. *How sick is that?* he wondered. Happy for the chance to have it out with her. Finally get the truth from her, if she was capable of it.

Yep. He was happy to have a reason to enter the fight.

"YOU'RE SURE?" Delia asked, holding the phone to her ear so hard her head hurt. She sat back on her massage table, still warm from the last client.

As soon as Daphne and her shoulder problems had left, Delia had called J.D., the private investigator, because the frustration and worry of her situation was fraying her composure.

She couldn't stay here any longer. But she couldn't move until she knew where Jared was.

"I'm totally sure," J.D. said, his confidence translating to her shaking knees. "I've collected most of the evidence I need and I have a meeting with the district attorney on Friday night."

Two nights from now. She could hold on for two nights.

"But Josie called Jared. He's got the number here," she said, speaking her biggest fear aloud.

"That may be," J.D. said, "but I have a guy watching him and he's not going anywhere."

"I can come home?" she said, stumbling slightly on the word *home*. Luklo, Texas, would never be her home. But it was Josie's home and she wanted to be there.

And Delia wanted desperately to be away from the Riverview Inn. And Max. And the teasing, fleeting sense of happiness that she'd felt here.

She wanted her little girl to feel secure. And if that meant Texas, then she'd go back in a heartbeat.

She'd forgotten, briefly, drunk on Max's smile and touch, what was important. Josie. That's all.

"Not yet," J.D. said. "Chris Groames is looking pretty fragile these days and I think his role in what happened to you is killing him. He may crack soon, which would make the case pretty open-and-shut. But, even without him, I would think after Friday you'll need to be here. The district attorney will want to talk to you and to your daughter."

"There's no way around that?" Delia asked. "For Josie?"

"Nope, I'm sorry. Dave Biggins, who was arrested as the driver of the van found in the desert, is denying all connection to Jared. I've found some people willing to testify otherwise, including the man who rented them the van and a border patrol officer who saw them together a week before the incident. But your daughter saw them together that night and you said she heard them fighting."

"Yes, but—"

"Look, Delia, I've got another call coming in. Just sit tight for another two days. I'll call you on Friday after I meet with the D.A."

"Okay." She sighed and hung up.

The CD she played of babbling brooks and chimes that was supposed to calm the nerves and open the mind sounded like cats fighting and she smacked the off button. There was nothing relaxed in her, nothing calm.

Her mind spun with dark thoughts and worry and fear.

Josie was changing. Right before Delia's eyes. It was as if the center of her was slowly rotting and Delia didn't know what to do, how to fix it.

Her little girl had thrown a shoe at her this morning. She was rolling her eyes at everything

Delia said. There wasn't a suggestion she could make that wouldn't get a sighed "Whatever" from Josie.

At least if they were in Texas, Josie would have school and friends. But what about Jared? And if he was arrested, how much more would the scandal hurt Josie?

And what would Delia do? Her friends had betrayed her and she would endure sideways looks at the grocery store for the rest of her life.

And what about Max? What would she do with these feelings in Texas? Where could she put them?

She stood and began stripping the table, pulling off the linens as if they had personally insulted her. The corners stuck and she yanked and yanked, lifting the table off one leg, but still it wouldn't give.

"Damn it!" she said, hurling the armful of white sheets to the ground.

"Delia?"

"Max?" She whirled, stunned to see him in her spa. Stunned and oddly grateful after the way she'd treated him.

His body filled the doorway and his presence filled the room, pushing out all other thought from her head but him and the memory of his touch.

It had only been two days since she'd shut the door in his face and a little over two weeks that she'd known him and yet—looking at him—she couldn't ignore the fact that she missed him.

She felt as if she'd known him for years.

"What are you doing here?" she asked, as if days ago she hadn't looked at him with open invitation.

His black eyes scanned the room, the green walls and the small feminine touches she'd added to make the space hers, to own the work she did here, the healing she hoped she brought to people. "The place looks nice," he said. "I've never been in here."

"Well," she said, "it's no unfinished shed in the woods, but I like it."

His lips quirked again and she felt the breeze of happiness, the bright ray of gladness he brought to her, just by being here and barely smiling.

And that wasn't good.

She'd be leaving and she didn't need any more pain in her life. Feeling more for this man and hoping he felt more for her would only hurt her when she was back in Texas.

"Was there something you needed?" she asked. She crossed her arms over her chest and gripped her biceps to keep her hands occupied so she wouldn't foolishly reach out for him.

This attraction was born out of her situation. She was a woman in danger, on the run, and this guy seemed as secure and rock solid as they came. That's all. It was infatuation and proximity.

It wasn't real.

It couldn't be.

He finished his perusal of the room and turned his eyes to her. She felt that gaze like a physical touch under her clothes along the skin he'd touched a few nights ago. And suddenly she felt naked. She felt naked and spread-eagled on a bar waiting for him.

"I wanted to talk to you about Josie," he said.

"Is she okay? What's wrong?"

"She's fine." He held out a calming hand. "She spent the day with me, but she's not handling what's happened between you and her father very well."

"I know."

"I think," he said, his tone all business, "it might help if she talked to her dad in some capacity."

"What?" she cried, horrified at the idea.

"She's got a lot of questions for him and a lot of anger about what he did and right now she's putting that anger on you."

"I know, but—" she shook her head "—she can't talk to him. Ever."

"*Ever?* Why?"

She paused, wondering if it was safe to tell him. She wanted to desperately. She was tired of carrying her load alone, but before she could say anything, he rolled his eyes.

"Fine." He threw his hands up in the air. "Forget

it, Delia. Keep your secrets. But all I've ever wanted to do was help you." He turned to go and she knew she should let him. She couldn't. Not like this.

She grabbed his arm before he cleared the doorway. "You were right," she said. "Jared is a cop, but he's in a lot of trouble. Not just the thing with me. It's so much bigger than that and I'm doing what I can, but I don't want to implicate you or get you in trouble. Believe me, Max."

He blinked, stone-faced. "I believe you. I just don't understand you."

"I know." She tried to smile, to ease the atmosphere between them. "I don't understand me these days."

"Alice tells me you're leaving." His voice was low and quiet, but she could feel his hurt feelings. Because hers hurt, too.

"I was never going to stay here forever," she confessed. "It was always going to be temporary."

"You couldn't let me in on that?"

"I didn't think…" She hadn't thought at all really. "I didn't think it would matter. I wasn't planning on becoming friends with you, Max."

"So, it's not a fresh start?" Sarcasm laced his words.

"I don't get a fresh start, Max. Not with my life this way. We should be able to go back to Texas soon," she said and suddenly from out of nowhere, she realized how much she'd lose when it came time to go.

She looked up at the lights, blinking her eyes. It wasn't about her. Or her happiness or something as ridiculous as job satisfaction or as important as this man standing next to her, reaching out to take her hand.

"If you don't want to go, don't go," he said, as if it were that simple, as if the world were filled with people doing what they wanted without compromise.

Ludicrous.

"I can't."

"You won't." The anger in his voice spun her head around. "Listen to yourself, Delia. You've lain down and given up what you wanted most of your life—"

"You don't know that," she cried, snatching her hand back.

"You told me that," he said, exasperated. "You were your parents' battleground. You stuck it out in your unhappy marriage for the sake of your daughter. And now you're going to go back to Texas for her, too. You're punishing yourself for leaving her with Jared. Like you're to blame for everything that happened."

"Don't be ridiculous," she said, though it was the utter truth.

"You're being ridiculous. Get up, do some fighting for what you want. Your daughter is young and she needs you and some friends and a good, steady diet of the truth. She'll be fine."

"She needs security," she countered.

"What about you, Delia? Don't you need security? Don't you think the two go hand in hand?"

"You don't know me," she said, refusing to believe that it would really be that easy. That she could just decide and put her foot down and not take into account every other single person's feelings.

"The hell I don't." He stepped closer to her. So close she breathed air that smelled like him. Tasted like him. The sensation was like brandy on an empty stomach. She went weak in the knees and soft in the head. "I knew you the moment you let me touch you. I knew you the second you opened your mouth. Just like you knew me. You knew me enough to come find me and force me to deal with Iris. You offered me forgetfulness, remember?"

Oh God, how could she forget?

"And it's the one thing I've wanted more than anything else the past two years."

"Stop," she said. She held up her hand and stepped away so the heat from his body wouldn't muddle her head anymore. "We barely know each other. I will grant you that we have a pretty profound connection, but I think it's born of the circumstances we're in."

"You don't think what you feel is real?" he asked.

"Do you?" she countered, completely unable to definitively answer the question. She felt interrogated, under fire. The cop in him was showing.

Suddenly, his aggression fled. The hard focus in his eyes vanished and his whole body seemed to be on pause, as if he were trying to turn around but the current was too strong. And she knew he was going to do something important to him. He was going to show her some skeleton he had in his closet and she held up her hand, desperate to stop him. She couldn't reciprocate. She couldn't be what he needed.

"The woman," he said, "whose son I shot."

"Don't, Max," she breathed.

"I have to. I can't keep this inside anymore. It's ripping me apart."

All the pain that she'd glimpsed in his eyes before he covered it with his careful indifference was out in the open. Whatever secrets this man had were deep, and keeping them was costing him too much. As much as she didn't want to know, she couldn't let him keep it inside anymore. Not now, not since she could see what it cost him.

"That woman's name was Nell, and I had convinced myself, stupidly, that I loved her."

Delia braced herself on the table behind her, her stomach falling to her feet. For both of them. The drone of bees started in her head, a static worse than anything she'd ever heard before.

Two women abused by their husbands. Two women he felt compelled to help. Two women he felt more for than he should.

Was he so blind to not see this resemblance?

"Nothing ever happened," he said. "I doubt she even knew how I felt, but I let myself get lost between wanting to help her and wanting to save her." He shook his head, laughing bitterly. "I made so many mistakes. I got way too involved with the family. I let her make decisions she never should have made and that boy's death is on my conscience in more ways than one." He took a deep breath and scratched at his chest as if he'd suddenly let down a heavy load. "It's so good to say that. To finally admit to it."

Her head reeled. The load this man carried was too much for anyone. He didn't deserve it, but she was proof that you don't get what you deserve in this life.

"It's always been easier to shoulder the blame," he said. "To hide instead of dealing with it." He smiled at her. "But I want to deal with it."

Oh God, he wanted to deal with it because of her. Couldn't he see what he was doing?

"Why are you telling me this?" she asked.

"Because I've never told anyone. And I want

to tell you. You said you wanted a fresh start. Well, so do I."

"Have you asked yourself why you want a fresh start with me?" she asked, her mouth dry.

"Constantly." He laughed. "You've lied to me. You're still hiding the truth. We've only known each other two weeks—"

"My husband abused me and I am struggling to take care of my kid," she interrupted when he couldn't see the writing on the wall. "Just like Nell. Don't you see a resemblance?"

She came to stand on her shaking legs. He had all but told her that his feelings for her were no more than what he had felt for this Nell. Proof of what she was saying. What they felt couldn't be real, not with so much against them.

"You love a damsel in distress. That's what's attracting you to me."

"No, it's not. Trust me."

He grabbed her hand, held her fingers hard, as if they were in a storm and in danger of being torn apart, which, Delia recognized, was exactly what was happening.

"I've thought about this. When you first told me about your husband it was the first thing I thought. It's happening again. But then the more I got to know you, the more I realized you're not like Nell. You're like me."

"What?"

"Nell was a victim. She was always going to be a victim, if not to her husband, then to her son and life. She wouldn't have been able to help herself, or her family. Much less me. That's not you."

It felt like her. It felt exactly like her.

"You're a fighter who isn't fighting. Just like me," he said. "We're paralyzed between what we want and what we need. You want to give Josie security but you need it for yourself first. And as long as you keep sacrificing that, Josie will never feel safe and you'll never be happy."

She leaned against the table, the wind knocked out of her. Was he right? Was it that simple?

"I'm a cop, Delia. It's all I've ever wanted to be and I've let that get taken away from me because I was too scared to fight for it. Your life is being taken away from you because you're too scared to fight."

She shook her head, not wanting to believe it.

"I want you, Delia. I want you and your warrior soul and your messed-up daughter and all your baggage. I want to fight for you."

He stopped, waiting for her to say something. But she had nothing to say. She was going back to Texas. She had Jared and the D.A. to deal with. She had an unhappy daughter to make happy. She had a life to rebuild.

Rebuild it here, a voice whispered in her head. *Do this. Make yourself happy.*

"I can't—" She sighed and shook her head, panicked.

"Of course not," he said, the light draining from his eyes.

Then he left.

THAT NIGHT Gabe and Max walked down the hallway to Patrick's room. Gabe carried three plates filled with steaks and baked potatoes, while Max had a bottle of Scotch, three glasses and a heavy heart.

"This should work," Gabe said.

"Rare steak and Scotch usually do," Max agreed. He felt buoyed by his brother, by the prospect of eating with his dad. By the Scotch he'd already had to drink.

Anything to distract himself from thoughts of Delia.

Gabe pounded on their father's door. "Open up, old man," he called through the wood. "We're not taking no for an answer."

The door opened just as Gabe was going to knock again and Patrick stood there, his flannel shirt unbuttoned over one of the white T-shirts he wore every day.

"Hey, boys," he said with a grin, running a hand through his hair. "Am I ever glad to see you."

"Well, if you're so glad," Gabe asked, shoving a plate at his father, "why have you been hiding?"

Patrick grabbed the plate and stepped out of the way to let Gabe and Max walk in. Max set the Scotch and glasses down on the table in the corner, pushing away the stacks of Patrick's clean laundry, and poured them each a glass.

"I've had some thinking to do," Patrick said. He sat on his tidy bed and took the tumbler that Max handed him. "And I needed to talk to your mother."

"Let's not call her that," Gabe said. He pulled up a chair, rested his feet on the dresser and stared, cutting into his T-bone. "Let's never call her that."

Patrick nodded. "Nonetheless, we needed to talk."

"And?" Gabe asked around a mouthful of steak. Max pushed his plate aside and concentrated on his Scotch. Concentrated on getting good and blind drunk.

Delia had offered forgetfulness then yanked it away when he needed it more than ever.

"And, we talked." Patrick shrugged and cut into his own dinner. Gabe kept eating, Max kept drinking, knowing in the end their dad would talk when he was ready. He always did.

"She's going to invite Jonah here," he finally said and Gabe sputtered in his Scotch.

"That's good," Max said, watching his ice cubes melt. "I'd like to meet him."

"That's my boy," Patrick said, smiling at him.

"What about—Iris?" Gabe asked. "When's she leaving?"

"She's not." Patrick sighed and Max thought Gabe's head might explode. "Jonah won't come unless she's here."

Gabe didn't say anything, but cut his meat with a bit more force than might be required on something already dead.

"You have to do what you have to do, Dad," Max said, and poured himself a little more Scotch.

Gabe and Dad both turned to stare at him. "You okay, son?"

"Great," he said, feeling the booze work on the muscles in his chest around his wounded heart. "Fresh start," he said.

"Does this have something to do with that pretty redhead that's here?" Patrick asked, his blue eyes twinkling.

"Psst, Dad." Gabe pretended to cut his knife along his throat, telling Dad to shut up.

"No." Max held up his hand. "It's okay. We can talk about it. And yes, it's because of Delia."

Gabe's mouth fell open and he set his plate down, picking up the tumbler he'd set at his feet. "You want to talk?" he asked, and took a swig.

"I don't want to," Max conceded. "But I need to."

He felt the waves of love from his father and brother and suddenly felt bad for Jonah. Jonah might have gotten the mom, but he missed out on these two men and these two men made Max's life worth living.

"I appreciate the way you've let me live and work here," he said to Gabe.

"You're my brother," Gabe replied, furrowing his brow. "I want you here."

"And I appreciate how you've let me do things my way. I know you have a lot of questions about the shooting." He stopped and realized that he no longer felt so fragile, so ready to splinter at the thought of what had happened two years ago.

Just saying the words once and already he felt he had a grip on it, that the past didn't rule his life anymore.

"In your own time, son," Patrick said.

Max set aside his Scotch and told them about Nell. About how his muddied feelings had soured his decision-making skills. He told them how the boy he'd shot had been so wrapped up in what he'd felt was his parents' betrayal, his mother's weakness and his father's abuse.

"I think," he said, staring at his hands, running his thumb over the callus on his left palm. "I think he was waiting for a chance to hurt his mom and when his dad showed up it just sent him over the edge. He had the gun under his bed. Loaded and ready for I don't know how long. But once he got it, once he cocked it, he didn't even look at his father. He just raged at Nell. She was crying, holding out her hands to him, begging him to put the gun down, and he just aimed it right at her. His eyes were dry as a bone and I knew this kid was going to do it. He was going to take out all of us. So—" he took a huge breath of air "—I shot him. I didn't wound him, I didn't relieve him of his weapon. I put a bullet in his chest."

"The boy needed counseling," Patrick said after a moment.

"He did and his mother refused to see it."

Not like Delia. Delia was well aware of what was happening with Josie. Max just hoped she dealt with it in time, in the right way.

"It's not your fault," Gabe said, having long since leaned forward in his chair.

"It's not all my fault," Max admitted. "Some of it is. And I'm going to deal with that."

"Good for you, son." Patrick stood and clapped Max on the shoulder and Max surprised him by wrapping his arms around him.

"I love you, Dad," he whispered in the older man's ear. "You are the best dad, and whatever you need to do with Iris and Jonah, I support you."

"Oh, for crying out loud," Gabe muttered, and Max felt his brother wrap his arms around both of them. "I support you, too. Both of you."

"Good," Max said, pushing away from the incredibly awkward first-ever group hug the Mitchell men had shared, and everyone went back to their seats, surreptitiously wiping their eyes and picking up their food. "Because I quit."

CHAPTER FIFTEEN

DELIA WOKE in a sudden blind panic. She couldn't breathe, and her heart rate was through the roof.

Josie.

In the dark she couldn't see the lump of her daughter on her bed and she was sure, in her bones, that the bed was empty.

"Jos?" she whispered. She flipped the covers off her legs and stepped over to pat down Josie's bed. Nothing. Her little girl was gone.

The digital clock flashed 3:00 a.m. and she whirled into action, grabbing her robe and throwing it over the T-shirt and old yoga pants she wore to bed then heading out the door.

She did not want to believe the worst. Frankly, had Jared found them, she doubted he'd sneak off in the night with Josie and miss an opportunity to hurt Delia.

But her heart still skipped and stuttered as she opened the door to their room. "Jos?" she called quietly down the hall.

No response.

She ran for the stairs. "Josie?" she asked in the empty, shadowed dining room. "Where are you?"

Oh, God, she might have run. Might have gone out to the clearing in the middle of the night in the freezing cold. She could be hiding, punishing Delia for her role in the collapse of her life.

Delia grabbed her coat from the hooks by the main door and hurried toward the kitchen and the back door and the cold December night, only to be brought up short by the sight of her daughter and Patrick Mitchell sitting on the kitchen counter eating ice cream.

"Hi," Patrick said, cheerful and welcoming as though it wasn't the middle of the night and Delia hadn't just aged twenty years. "Your daughter and I seem to have the same late-night ice-cream cravings."

Josie put down her bowl, the spoon clanging against the porcelain as she leaped off the counter. The tennis shoes on her bare feet and her winter coat tossed on the butcher block told a different story than ice-cream craving.

She'd been about to run off but Patrick stopped her.

Delia gasped for air.

"Calm down, Mom," Josie said, her patronizing tone ugly out of her eight-year-old mouth.

Delia's mind was a blank for a strong, motherly comeback. She didn't know what to say, or do.

"Why don't you go get your daughter settled," Patrick said, when it was clear she wasn't going to be able to say anything.

"Right," Delia breathed. She held out her hand, grazing Josie's shoulder, but her daughter jerked away, walking toward the kitchen door with her head high like some kind of noble prisoner of war.

"Come back." Patrick's low voice followed Delia out the door. "When she's asleep."

They returned to their room and Delia tried to figure out what approach to take with this stranger living in her daughter's body.

When Josie finally pushed open the door to the room, Delia had decided, since everything else failed, she'd have a go with honesty.

"Were you going to run away?" she asked Josie, who only shrugged blithely with one shoulder.

"I am trying to be calm, Josie, but you are beginning to scare me. What is going on?" Moonlight sliced a white triangle from the center of Josie's face and she appeared to be made of stone.

"I was just going to go outside," she said.

"It's the middle of the night," Delia cried. "And it's freezing."

"I know."

Josie's head tilted as she looked down at her hands and Delia could finally see her eyes, dry and solemn.

"Do you think Dad is coming here?"

"I don't know, sweetie."

Josie sighed. "A little girl came over yesterday," she said. "Helen."

"I know. Her mom came in for a massage."

"Helen and I helped Max with his fort."

"That must have been fun."

"I pushed her down in the snow," she said, and Delia's blood ran cold. This was why Max came to her yesterday, the problems he said Josie was having. Oh, God, she never saw this kind of behavior coming. A quiver started in her blood, ran through her organs and made her whole body shake.

She felt as if someone had turned off the lights and she stood in utter darkness, unsure of direction. Unsure even of which way was up.

"Why did you do that?" she asked carefully.

Josie shrugged.

"Remember what we told you about hurting people?" Delia said firmly, despite the quaking. She sat on the edge of Josie's bed, wanting desperately to shake her daughter until she told her what she was feeling, what was going on. "You know better than to do that kind of thing."

"Dad did it," Josie said, her little face fierce in the moonlight.

"And Dad was wrong and he's going to be punished. And get in a lot of trouble, Josie." She stood, angry at the mention of Jared's name. "Tomorrow we're going to go over to Daphne and Helen's house and apologize."

"I already did," she said, staring back out the window. "I felt bad for doing it."

"Of course you did, Josie. Because it's a bad thing to do."

"I'll bet Dad doesn't feel bad."

The shaking stopped and, like a door opening, she saw what Josie was thinking and her heart broke for her baby.

Delia leaned over Josie's bed and touched her daughter's chin, forcing her to look at her. "You aren't your dad," she said. "You're you. And you're scared and hurt right now, but you are a good girl. You are smart and kind and funny, and kids like you don't do things like that."

"Daddy always told me I was just like him," Josie said and Delia got down on her knees beside her daughter's bed, feeling an ugly crossroads at work in her daughter.

"You're like you. That's it. You've got some of him in you, and you've got some of me in you, but mostly you're you. And you are a good person."

Josie took a long time to think about it then she turned her face away, looking back out the window. "I won't sneak out again, Mom," she said. "I'm sorry I scared you."

"I love you, Josie," Delia said, and kissed Josie's forehead, something she hadn't done in months because she'd seemed so reluctant to be touched.

"I know, Mom," Josie said, and patted her cheek. She even smiled a little, but Delia felt no closer to her daughter.

Delia stayed there, stroking Josie's hair until she finally fell asleep again. Then, restless and at loose ends, she went downstairs to see if Patrick was still up.

He was and when she stepped into the kitchen he reached over to the freezer and pulled out a pint of Ben & Jerry's to hand to her. "We seem to have a lot of this stuff around," he said. "One of the benefits of having a pregnant woman in house."

"Better she crave ice cream than spinach," Delia joked, taking the ice cream. "For you, I mean." He laughed and she was suddenly so glad to be down here rather than up in that room, staring at her sleeping daughter.

"That's some little girl you've got there," Patrick said. His voice seemed somehow knowing and respectful at the same time, and she remembered that he'd been a single father to two headstrong boys. He must have had plenty of sleepless nights.

"She's been through a lot." She grabbed a spoon

and hoisted herself up on the counter where her daughter had sat.

"She was on her way out the door to my son's shed when I found her," he said. "She reminds me of him. Still waters and all that."

"I think it's why my daughter took to him so fast," she said, spooning out some chocolate ice cream. "They were friends in the first ten minutes she spent with him. I spent the first five years of her life despairing that she'd ever have friends."

"Sounds like Max all right." Patrick smiled, looking deep into his own pint. "You and your daughter really worked some magic on him."

The ice cream in her mouth suddenly turned to sludge. She didn't want to think about Max. She'd come to grips with her decision and if she didn't think about him, if she locked away those fledgling feelings she had for him, she couldn't regret the decision.

She wanted to laugh off Patrick's compliment, minimize what had happened between her and Max, but she couldn't. She didn't know how, when she was still wrestling with the size and scope of what had happened, herself.

"When I left here, it was the same Max I'd been worrying about for the past two years. And when I come back—" He shook his head, smiling sadly. "Well, I just never thought I'd see that part of my boy again. Smiling. Talking. You know he never told anyone about the details of the shooting?" His eyes sparkled with tears in the half-light of the kitchen. "Gabe and I tried for months to get him to talk to us. Talk to his old partner on the force. Anyone. And no dice. He shut us out."

"I'm glad he's talking again," she managed to say. "He's a special man."

"I know we don't know each other and maybe you'll want to slap me in the face, but I know my son and I know love when I see it." His eyes pinned her to the wall. "And he's not the only one who feels it."

"I'm not staying," she said quickly, her voice a mere breath of longing. "I can't. My daughter—"

He held up his hand. "Say no more, I understand wanting to protect your kids." He laughed, but it wasn't happy. "I did it my whole life."

The words were rich with regret, covered in remorse, and she couldn't help but imagine herself in thirty years, alone in a kitchen with only Ben & Jerry for company. Her child grown and finding her own life and loves.

That's okay, she told herself, thinking of her daughter upstairs, so fragile and wounded. *It will be worth it if she's okay.*

Patrick spun the cardboard pint in a slow circle on the butcher block he leaned against. "Our kids learn so much from us. How to read. How to behave. How to think about the world. But you know what I just figured out. They also learn how to be happy from us."

Delia felt all the hair on her neck stand up.

"I'm not sure if you noticed, but Max has a hard time with happy, and Gabe, before Alice came back in his life—" He whistled. "It was like he was copying me trying to be happy."

Delia set down her own ice cream, her throat closed. *I will be happy again,* she told herself, willing herself to believe it. *Just not right now. Now is not my time.*

Max is not for me.

"Your daughter might not be able to put it into words, but she wants you to be happy," he murmured, and she felt his hand on her shoulder, heavy with experience and wisdom. "She wants you to be happy so she can be happy."

He patted her and kissed her forehead. "You're a good kid," he said, and left, leaving his words behind him to reconfigure her life.

DAY ONE of Max's fresh start was already better because Alice had made coffee.

"Hey," she said, not rising up from Gabe's cushioned rolling office chair she'd pulled up to the big chopping block in the kitchen. "I heard there was a Mitchell family love-in last night and I wasn't invited."

"Sorry, men group hugs only." He smiled at her and poured some coffee into his travel mug.

"Gabe says you're doing better."

"I am." He leaned over and pressed a kiss to her forehead, while she gaped, astonished. "I am going to apply for a juvenile parole officer position."

"Good for you." She smiled. "You shouldn't waste your talents building mysterious sheds in the woods."

"You're probably right." He laughed, feeling lighter than he had in years. Not just since the shooting, or meeting Nell. Further back than that. Maybe since he was a boy.

And unbelievably, he had Delia to thank for it.

And blame for his lagging heart.

The phone rang and Alice went to answer it, rolling herself to the office.

Max turned to leave, planning on going into town to talk to Joe about that job, only to end up opening the door for Joe as he walked in, shaking snow off his hat and stomping his feet.

"Sheriff," he said, "I was just coming to talk to you—"

Joe held up a hand and Max got a good look at his dead-serious eyes. "We've got a problem," he said.

"LISTEN, JOSIE," Delia said, crossing her arms over her chest and getting in her daughter's face. It had been a long night, Patrick's and Max's words echoing through her head until dawn crept through the window.

She'd stared at the new light, fresh and pink and decided to stay. And fight.

For her daughter. For her feelings for Max.

For happiness.

If Max could work toward forgiving his mother, she could forgive herself for taking care of her own. For leaving Josie with Jared when she'd had no idea what would come of it.

Delia didn't deserve to be unhappy for the rest of her life.

She deserved the Riverview Inn. She deserved Max.

"You are a child. You are my child and I have tried to make you happy," she said, smiling. "I have tried to talk to you and give you distance. But nothing has worked."

Josie sat on the end of the bed looking chagrined and that gave Delia hope. That and the echo of Max's words telling her that her little girl only needed her, some friends and a steady diet of the truth.

"We have some choices to make," she said. "And I will tell you the truth if you tell me the truth."

Josie seemed intent on picking her thumbnail, but she didn't say no so Delia took that as a good sign.

"We can go back to Texas, try and pick up our lives—"

"Without Dad?"

Delia sighed. "Dad might be in jail, Josie."

"What's our other choice?"

"We can move someplace else. North Carolina, maybe?"

"Or?"

"Or we can stay here." She crouched down in front of her baby and waited until their eyes met. "And I want to stay."

She waited. Josie didn't say anything and Delia began to realize it was too much for an eight-year-old. That, by once again trying to be fair, or reasonable or not scar her further, Delia was making things harder for Josie.

What eight-year-old could make that kind of decision?

"I want to stay here with you," Delia declared, shoving those divorce books out of her mind. She trusted herself enough to do things her way. "I'm not asking your permission," she said. "But I want to know that you are happy. That we're in this together?"

But again, Josie didn't answer, and Delia

wondered if she'd ever have a loving relationship with her little girl.

There was a knock on the door and Delia turned, hoping against hope that it might be Max. Because he showed up that way, in her worst moment, when she was flailing about like some kind of beached whale on the shore of her indecision.

And the thought of Max cemented her decision.

They were going to stay. They had a family of sorts here. Friends. Work she loved. A man she might grow to love.

"Hi." Gabe stuck his head around the door, holding on to a cordless phone. "Sorry to interrupt, but Alice answered a phone call for you and she sent me up here to make sure you got it. The man says it's urgent."

Josie was ashen, her fingers clenched in her lap.

"Did you call Dad?" Delia asked, feeling panic like a flood drowning her.

Josie shook her head and the fear in her eyes told Delia she was being truthful.

She reached out for the cordless and thanked Gabe as he ducked back into the hallway.

"Hello?" she said, hating that her voice trembled.

"Delia? It's J.D." J.D. sounded close to panicked and instinctively she wrapped her arm around her daughter, comforted and relieved when Josie clung to her.

"What's wrong?"

"My guy lost Jared about twelve hours ago."

"Lost? What do you mean 'lost'?"

"I mean we don't know where he is. I've talked to the D.A. A warrant for his arrest was issued yesterday and he ran. The guy I had following him was found unconscious and nearly beaten to death in Missouri just a few hours ago. Doing the math, we think he's been on the road for twelve hours."

She felt Jared's thumb against her windpipe as if he was trying to kill her all over again. She couldn't breathe. Couldn't think.

"Is he coming here?" she breathed, clutching Josie to her side.

"My gut says yes. I need you to get out of there. Get someplace safe. I have contacted the local police and he's on his way to the inn right now. But for your own safety I can only advise you to leave the premises."

"Right," she said. Leave. Again. Keep running. Just when she'd gathered the courage to stay. Her whole body shook with how wrong that was. "I'll be in touch."

She hit End on the phone and threw it behind her.

"What's going on?" Josie asked, white-faced and scared.

"I'm not sure yet." She took a deep breath and took her daughter by the shoulders, holding her gaze so she understood that she was serious. Whatever breakdown was going on in Josie's head needed to be put on hold for the moment, while the natural parent-child order was restored. "We might have to leave, but for right now, I want you to stay in here. I need you to lock the door and only answer it when you hear me or Max."

"Max?"

"That's it. You keep it shut for everyone else." She stroked her daughter's hair back from her face. "Especially Daddy."

"O-okay." Josie nodded and Delia pulled her into her arms, kissing her temple, holding her little bones as close as possible. "I love you, baby. I am going to try and do the right thing."

Josie nodded then Delia left, turning the knob on the door to make sure Josie locked it.

"Good girl," she called through the wood when the doorknob didn't turn all the way.

She went to find Max.

JOE HANDED Max a gun. "I'm not sure what we're up against here," he said. "But that P.I. I talked to made it sound like this guy was capable of anything."

The black Beretta, standard issue for country

sheriffs, was a living thing in his palm. A snake. An angry scorpion.

"I—" Max shook his head, hesitant to step back into these shoes.

"Max?" Gabe, his brother, beloved and scared shitless, stood beside him. "Man, I think we need you to take that gun."

Right. *We.* Lots of innocent people. And he might be the only thing between them and a madman.

Max took the gun, shaking off the ghosts that clung to him. He checked the clip and tucked the gun in the back of his pants, nestling it up against his spine.

"I need you to get everyone to their rooms," Max said to Gabe. "Get them there and keep them there. I don't need any more innocent bystanders in the way."

Gabe nodded and took off at a run to do what needed to be done.

"Call for some backup," Max told Joe. "I've got to talk to Delia."

Joe left and Max ran through the kitchen, flinging open the door and charging through the dining room. He had started up the stairs when she appeared. Just like that.

Standing at the top of the stairs, her face pale and eyes blazing, he knew she was aware of what was happening.

"My husband is on his way here," she said.

"We think he might be at the state line," he told her. "Joe's got state troopers looking for him, but there are so many county highways we have no idea—"

"I don't want to run anymore," she said, and Max realized that as fragile as she appeared, as shaken and freaked-out, there was something else at work here, something giving her height and depth. Suddenly she seemed bigger, taller. Stronger. "But my daughter—"

"We'll keep her safe," he said. "I won't let anything happen to her. We can get you to a safe house."

"What's safe?" she asked. "My family? My home? I've let him take all of that from me."

Though he wanted to be unmoved, his heart shook for her. Firm in his righteous anger at her earlier inability to fully understand what she was throwing away when she refused to fight for what she wanted.

"But I'm not going to let him take you from me, Max. I just told Josie I wanted to stay," she said. "I want to stay here, with you, with your family and now he could take that away from me, too."

"You're scared," he said, wanting to believe her but knowing she was too spun around to understand what she was saying. "These are things we can talk about later, when you're able to think clearly."

"I *am* thinking clearly," she told him. "I am thinking more clearly right now than I have in maybe my whole life. That's crazy, isn't it?" She took the steps down until she stood a heartbeat from him and took his face between her hands. "I am going to have to leave. I have to keep my daughter safe, but I want you to know that I want you, too. I want your scars and your loneliness and your messed-up family and your talented hands. I want your noble heart and your infrequent smiles."

He opened his mouth to tell her that she didn't need to say these things. That the unpredictability of the moment was making her say things she didn't mean, but she kissed him.

She pressed one hard and fast kiss against his lips. Her fingers touched his scar, her hand cupped his cheek and, for a moment, a split second, he let himself believe her.

"Very sweet," an ugly voice sneered and Delia spun so fast Max put a hand to her waist to keep her steady.

A tall man, well built, with twenty-four hours of beard on his face and enough menace in his eyes to make Max grab his gun, stood at the top of the stairs with Josie under his arm.

Jared.

CHAPTER SIXTEEN

"JOSIE—" Delia cried, and lunged for her, but Max held her back. He was too strong to overpower, but he had to give her credit.

"Are you okay, Jos?" Max asked, and Josie, her face wan and covered in tears, nodded slowly.

He felt the past rush up and fill the room. Suddenly there were two women. Too many children. Too many guns. Too many factors that could make everything go wrong.

The scars along his neck and in his thigh went white-hot as if to remind him of his failures. Pointing out the terrible fact that he'd been here before with terrible results.

I can't do it. I can't keep everyone safe.

"*Jos?*" Jared asked, mildly mocking. "Who the hell are you calling my daughter nicknames?"

"He's Max," Josie murmured.

"Max?" Jared smiled, a wolf bearing his teeth, and a chill swept down Max's spine. This guy was bad news. "You're Max Mitchell? The cop who shot that teenager?" He shook his head, tsking his tongue. "Not good for business, man," he said. "It's a good thing you left the force. We don't need men like you in the brotherhood."

Two days ago Jared's words would have wounded Max. Would have made his hand tremble and his head second-guess.

But Delia grabbed his hand where he held her shirt and that touch, strong, steady and fierce, cleared the room, banished the demons and lent steadiness where he needed it.

She needed him and he wouldn't let her down.

"You're not my brother," Max muttered.

"He's my friend," Josie said, her little fingers stretching out to him.

Oh, Jos, he thought. *You're my friend, too.*

"No." Jared jerked Josie back, a little too violently for a loving father and the dangerous unpredictability escalated. A weapon had not materialized, but Max was sure it would when Jared was provoked enough. "He's not your friend, Josie."

Delia pulled away again, but Max kept her close. If there were going to be bullets, he needed to know he could get her out of the way.

And he would. He'd die protecting these girls. His girls.

"I FOUND our little girl in the hallway eavesdropping," Jared said.

Delia's skin crawled. Her head buzzed with fear and she couldn't make sense of what was happening. How could Jared be here? How could he be touching Josie that way?

"She's picked up some bad habits on this little mother-daughter vacation of yours."

"Jared, there are a lot of cops on their way with a warrant for your arrest," Max said, and his voice was so calm it allowed Delia to think. It allowed her to trust him. Everything was going to be okay. Max was here.

"Let them come," Jared said expansively, his brown eyes glowing with a scary kind of insanity that Delia had never seen before.

"The investigator you hired hasn't got anything," Jared said.

He had to be lying. Please, God, let him be lying. There has to be a way out of this.

"Just a vanload of dead bodies, Jared. You can't hide—"

"What do you want, Jared?" Max asked.

"I want my daughter!" Jared yelled, edging ever closer to some breaking point. He gripped Josie's shoulder hard enough that she cried out and Delia reached for her, straining past Max, wanting her little girl safe in her arms. "She belongs with me."

"Over my dead—" Delia cried.

"That's not going to happen, Jared," Max interrupted.

"Oh no?" He crouched down, stroking Josie's shoulders, clearly impervious to how much he was scaring her. Delia's own skin crawled when he touched Josie. "Do you want to go home, sweetie?" he asked. "Do you want to come home with me?"

Delia sucked in a breath and felt the world spin. She clutched Max for support, no longer trying to get past him.

What if Josie said yes?

Even with all that had happened, despite her efforts to be a good mother, the right kind of mother, Josie could still choose her father. Time stopped and Delia felt the weight of Josie's decision in every single fiber of her muscle. Tears rolled down her face and she prayed incoherently, her heart breaking with every second and still Josie said nothing.

Josie looked at her father, her young eyes searching the devils in Jared's and finally Delia could not take it another moment. She put her head down on Max's shoulder.

"Baby," she whispered. "My baby. I'm so sorry."

"Mom?" Josie cried. Delia's head came up.

"Josie?"

"Mom!"

Jared wrapped an arm around his daughter's waist and lifted her, kicking and screaming, into the air.

"I want my mom!"

"You can't have her," Jared said, and pulled a gun from his waistband.

"Josie!" Delia screamed.

Max crouched, holding his gun with one hand and Delia with the other. "Drop the weapon," he demanded. "You don't want to do anything you'll regret."

Jared trained his weapon on Delia. The sound of a chamber loading filled the room and Delia looked down the barrel of that gun, knowing sanity had left the building.

Max will keep me safe, she thought, paralyzed, repeating it like a mantra.

"Josie," Max said, cocking the weapon. "Close your eyes."

Josie clenched her eyes shut tight and Max pulled the trigger.

Jared fell, screaming, the gun falling from his hand. Delia charged up the stairs and grabbed her daughter, whirling her away from the blood and Jared's screams of pain.

Josie buried her face in Delia's neck and her whole body sobbed in relief. "I've got you, baby, I've got you," she said, holding her as tight as she could.

"Don't let me go," Josie whimpered.

"Never," Delia vowed, and ran to their room.

JARED MADE A GRAB for the gun, but Max kicked it out of reach and stepped on Jared's hand with his boot heel. Jared's screams hit a new pitch of pain.

Max wanted to break every bone in Jared's body. Break every finger that had brought pain and violence to Delia's life. But he contented himself by mashing that hand deeper into the carpet.

With his good hand, Jared gripped his shattered knee to his chest, blood oozing through his fingers, cartiledge littering the carpet under him.

Gabe was not going to be happy about that, Max thought, putting the gun back in the waist of his pants, feeling the cop in him return.

"What the hell is wrong with you?" Jared gasped. "I'm a cop."

"No," Max shook his head. "You're not."

The man he used to be slowly returned, filling his skin and his muscles with his old sense of duty. Of obligation. Of right and wrong.

"*I'm* a cop," he said. Testing the words as Joe and his men streamed into the lodge.

TEN MINUTES AFTER the shooting and Josie still trembled. Delia stroked her hair, and her back. She cooed and whispered as much comfort as she could into her daughter's ear, but the trembling didn't stop. She didn't think it ever would.

"It's over, Josie," she murmured.

"Is Dad dead?"

"No, honey. Max shot him in the knee. You were so brave to do what he asked and keep your eyes shut."

"He scared me, Mom."

Delia sighed. "I know, honey, but Max was just trying to keep—"

"Not Max." Josie lifted her head. Her face was red and swollen, her eyes puffy. "Dad scared me."

Delia pulled her back against her shoulder, holding her as tight as possible. "Well, he can't anymore," she said.

There was a knock at the door and, instead of getting up or moving her daughter from her arms, she just yelled, "Come in."

Max entered, white-faced and serious.

"Are you okay?" he asked. She could tell, because she knew him so well, that he was consumed with worry that he'd hurt Josie. That he'd sent her further into her tailspin.

"We're okay," Delia said.

"Max?" Josie lifted her head, the tears starting fresh. "Max—" She reached for him and Max's austere face crumpled, his eyes flooded with moisture and he was on his knees in front of them, hugging them both.

"So brave," he said, pushing Josie's hair from her face. "You're such a brave little girl." He pressed a kiss to her forehead then turned to look at Delia. "I know you were scared and you didn't know what you were saying before Jared showed up." He gripped her leg. "But I'm taking you at your word," he said. "You want to stay."

She looked at Josie and saw her small nod against Max's shoulder.

They were all slowly mending those broken spots inside themselves and promises now would be foolish. But she wanted to stay. She wanted to see where this would go.

There was uncertainty in his eyes that he couldn't hide. Feelings that echoed her own.

What happens next?

Is this real?

"One day at a time," she told him, pressing a kiss to his neck, just beneath his scar. "Let's take it one day at a time."

CHAPTER SEVENTEEN

"NONE OF MY OTHER friends have to go to counseling," Josie groused, staring out the passenger-door window.

She was nine going on thirty and Delia could only hold her breath and pray that somehow she would just skip the teenage years.

"Well, I doubt your friends have gone through what you've had to go through," she said, turning off the highway onto the gravel road that led to the front door of the Riverview Inn.

The gravel road that led them home.

Seven months at the Riverview and it was more home, the Mitchells more family, than either she or Josie had ever experienced.

"You like it here?" she asked Josie, and her daughter predictably rolled her eyes.

"Yes, Mom. How many times do I have to tell you?"

"Just checking," she said, smiling. They were

happy. The three of them, an unorthodox family. Her, Josie and Max.

They hit the bump in the road, turned the corner and there was the inn.

"You think Chef Tim made shish kebabs?" Josie asked.

"Ah, yeah," Delia joked. "He makes them every Tuesday. Just for you."

Josie grinned and watched the world outside the window.

Finally, Delia parked the car and Max came out the back door, grinning. Oh, he was a handsome man when he smiled.

And while a juvenile parole officer didn't wear a uniform, she imagined he would be back in uniform when Joe retired next year.

She had to admit, she looked forward to seeing her handsome man in uniform.

"Hey, Max!" Josie yelled out the window, all of her preteen attitude gone at his arrival.

"Hey, kid," he said, opening the driver door and helping Delia out of the car. "Hey, lady," he whispered, and gave her a warm, full kiss.

"Hello, Officer," she breathed back.

He wrapped his arm around her and shut the car door. "Follow me," he said, leading her toward the trail leading back to his old shed.

"Me, too?" Josie asked.

"Especially you," he said, and like the nine-year-old she was, she ran on ahead.

"What are you doing?" Delia asked, loving the twinkle in his eye. The strength of his arm around her waist.

"You'll see."

Josie stood at the edge of the clearing, staring at the shed.

"What'd you do?" she asked, looking back at Max.

"I finished it," he said. "Finally."

"But are you going to put lawn mowers in that?" Josie asked. "It's so pretty."

Delia looked around Josie and saw that not only was the shed finished, but it was painted purple. Bright purple. With a red door.

And he'd cut windows in his shed.

"Go check it out," he said, nudging Josie. "There's some stuff inside."

Josie ran off and Delia turned to face him, astonished and in love. Deeply in love. She stood there, a new woman, with all her love for him.

"It's just some art stuff," he said, watching the shed and smiling when they heard Josie whoop. "You said the counselor believed that the art therapy was working. And—" he laughed "—a

CD player so I don't have to listen to Justin Timberlake anymore. A couple of sudoku puzzles. A little surprise for—"

"Marry me," she said, interrupting. She wasn't joking—it wasn't something they joked about.

He smiled, slow and sweet, and her whole body quivered with desire and affection. "You have to make an honest woman out of me," she said.

"I've been trying," he told her. "But you put up quite a fight."

"I thought you liked that," she murmured, twining her arms around his neck. He reached under the hem of her shirt and stroked her back.

"Mom!" Josie screamed, and came tearing out the door holding a blue box. "You have got to see this!"

Josie hurled herself against them and pressed the blue box—the blue ring box—into her hand.

Delia blinked up at the love of her life and joy washed over her like a river. Unending. Consuming.

"You beat me to the punch," he murmured.

Delia tipped her head back and laughed. She laughed until tears ran down her cheeks and Max joined her, his chuckle startling birds from trees.

"Are we getting married?" Josie asked, hugging their waists tight. Max reached down and cupped

Josie's head, smiling at her as though he could never love her more.

"You bet we are," Delia said, holding tight to her man worth keeping.

* * * * *

Don't miss the next book in
THE MITCHELLS OF RIVERVIEW INN
series
by Molly O'Keefe
Coming in August 2008
from Harlequin Superromance

Look for LAST WOLF WATCHING
by Rhyannon Byrd—the exciting conclusion
in the BLOODRUNNERS miniseries
from Silhouette Nocturne.

Follow Michaela and Brody on their fierce
journey to find the truth and face the demons
from the past, as they reach the heart of the
battle between the Runners and the rogues.

Here is a sneak preview of book three,
LAST WOLF WATCHING.

Michaela squinted, struggling to see through the impenetrable darkness. Everyone looked toward the Elders, but she knew Brody Carter still watched her. Michaela could feel the power of his gaze. Its heat. Its strength. And something that felt strangely like anger, though he had no reason to have any emotion toward her. Strangers from different worlds, brought together beneath the heavy silver moon on a night made for hell itself. That was their only connection.

The second she finished that thought, she knew it was a lie. But she couldn't deal with it now. Not tonight. Not when her whole world balanced on the edge of destruction.

Willing her backbone to keep her upright, Michaela Doucet focused on the towering blaze of a roaring bonfire that rose from the far side of the clearing, its orange flames burning with maniacal zeal against the inky black curtain of the night. Many of the Lycans had already shifted into their preternatural shapes, their fur-covered bodies standing like monstrous shadows at the edges of the forest as they waited with restless expectancy for her brother.

Her nineteen-year-old brother, Max, had been attacked by a rogue werewolf—a Lycan who preyed upon humans for food. Max had been bitten in the attack, which meant he was no longer human, but a breed of creature that existed between the two worlds of man and beast, much like the Bloodrunners themselves.

The Elders parted, and two hulking shapes emerged from the trees. In their wolf forms, the Lycans stood over seven feet tall, their legs bent at an odd angle as they stalked forward. They each held a thick chain that had been wound around their inside wrists, the twin lengths leading back into the shadows. The Lycans had taken no more than a few steps when they jerked on the chains, and her brother appeared.

Bound like an animal.

Biting at her trembling lower lip, she glanced

left, then right, surprised to see that others had joined her. Now the Bloodrunners and their family and friends stood as a united force against the Silvercrest pack, which had yet to accept the fact that something sinister was eating away at its foundation—something that would rip down the protective walls that separated their world from the humans'. It occurred to Michaela that loyalties were being announced tonight—a separation made between those who would stand with the Runners in their fight against the rogues and those who blindly supported the pack's refusal to face reality. But all she could focus on was her brother. Max looked so hurt...so terrified.

"Leave him alone," she screamed, her soft-soled, black satin slip-ons struggling for purchase in the damp earth as she rushed toward Max, only to find herself lifted off the ground when a hard, heavily muscled arm clamped around her waist from behind, pulling her clear off her feet. "Damn it, let me down!" she snarled, unable to take her eyes off her brother as the golden-eyed Lycan kicked him.

Mindless with heartache and rage, Michaela clawed at the arm holding her, kicking her heels against whatever part of her captor's legs she could reach. "Stop it," a deep, husky voice grunted in her ear. "You're not helping him by losing it. I give you my word he'll survive the ceremony, but you have to keep it together."

"Nooooo!" she screamed, too hysterical to listen to reason. "You're monsters! All of you! Look what you've done to him! How dare you! *How dare you!*"

The arm tightened with a powerful flex of muscle, cinching her waist. Her breath sucked in on a sharp, wailing gasp.

"Shut up before you get both yourself and your brother killed. I will *not* let that happen. Do you understand me?" her captor growled, shaking her so hard that her teeth clicked together. "Do you understand me, Doucet?"

"Damn it," she cried, stricken as she watched one of the guards grab Max by his hair. Around them Lycans huffed and growled as they watched the spectacle, while others outright howled for the show to begin.

"That's enough!" the voice seethed in her ear. "They'll tear you apart before you even reach him, and I'll be damned if I'm going to stand here and watch you die."

Suddenly, through the haze of fear and agony and outrage in her mind, she finally recognized who'd caught her. *Brody*.

He held her in his arms, her body locked against his powerful form, her back to the burning heat of his chest. A low, keening sound of anguish tore through her, and her head dropped forward as hoarse sobs of pain ripped from her throat. "Let me go. I have to help him. *Please,*" she begged brokenly, knowing only that she needed to get to Max. "Let me go, Brody."

He muttered something against her hair, his breath warm against her scalp, and Michaela could have sworn it was a single word…. But she must have heard wrong. She was too upset. Too furious. Too terrified. She must be out of her mind.

Because it sounded as if he'd quietly snarled the word *never*.

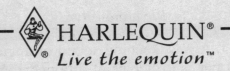

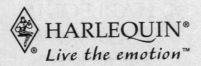

HARLEQUIN®
INTRIGUE®

BREATHTAKING ROMANTIC SUSPENSE

Shared dangers and passions lead to electrifying
romance and heart-stopping suspense!

Every month, you'll meet six new heroes
who are guaranteed to make your spine tingle
and your pulse pound. With them you'll enter
into the exciting world of Harlequin Intrigue—
where your life is on the line
and so is your heart!

THAT'S INTRIGUE—
ROMANTIC SUSPENSE
AT ITS BEST!

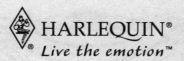

HARLEQUIN®
Live the emotion™

Harlequin® Historical
Historical Romantic Adventure!

Imagine a time of chivalrous knights and unconventional ladies, roguish rakes and impetuous heiresses, rugged cowboys and spirited frontierswomen—these rich and vivid tales will capture your imagination!

*Harlequin Historical...
they're too good to miss!*

HHDIR06

HARLEQUIN®
Presents

The world's bestselling romance series...
The series that brings you your favorite authors,
month after month:

Helen Bianchin...Emma Darcy
Lynne Graham...Penny Jordan
Miranda Lee...Sandra Marton
Anne Mather...Carole Mortimer
Susan Napier...Michelle Reid

and many more uniquely talented authors!

Wealthy, powerful, gorgeous men...
Women who have feelings just like your own...
The stories you love, set in exotic, glamorous locations...

HARLEQUIN®
Presents

Seduction and Passion Guaranteed!

HPDIR104

✔ *Silhouette*®

SPECIAL EDITION™

**Emotional, compelling
stories that capture the
intensity of living, loving
and creating a family in
today's world.**

Special Edition features bestselling
authors such as Susan Mallery,
Sherryl Woods, Christine Rimmer,
Joan Elliott Pickart—
and many more!

For a romantic, complex
and emotional read, choose
Silhouette Special Edition.

✔ *Silhouette*®